"I don't know what I'm doing."

A gentle smile lifted Merritt's mouth, and her charming dimples appeared. "Then that's a different story entirely. Anyone can learn."

"Would you stay to help? I can pay you—"

"I don't want your money, Knox." Her smile disappeared, but her features were still soft. "But I will stay, if you really want me to, and help you learn what you need to know."

"You'd do that for me?" He hadn't thought Merritt would want to help him after what happened with her sister.

"I'd do it for all of you." She tilted her head toward the door where Addy had disappeared. "Those girls need you, more than anything else. More than a good nanny, presents or even this ginormous house. They need their daddy, and if you want to be there for them, I would love to help you do that."

Warmth filled his chest at her words. Her selflessness was not what he had anticipated. He couldn't assume that Merritt was like her sister.

Yet he wouldn't let his guard down, either. He'd been hurt too deeply to trust anyone again— especially a Lane sister.

Gabrielle Meyer lives in central Minnesota on the banks of the Mississippi River with her husband and four young children. As an employee of the Minnesota Historical Society, she fell in love with the rich history of her state and enjoys writing fictional stories inspired by real people and events. Gabrielle can be found at www.gabriellemeyer.com, where she writes about her passion for history, Minnesota and her faith.

Books by Gabrielle Meyer

Love Inspired

A Mother's Secret
Unexpected Christmas Joy
A Home for Her Baby
Snowed in for Christmas
Fatherhood Lessons

Visit the Author Profile page at LoveInspired.com for more titles.

Fatherhood Lessons

Gabrielle Meyer

LOVE INSPIRED

INSPIRATIONAL ROMANCE

LOVE INSPIRED®
INSPIRATIONAL ROMANCE

PLEASE RECYCLE
THIS PRODUCT IS RECYCLABLE

Recycling programs
for this product may
not exist in your area.

ISBN-13: 978-1-335-75913-9

Fatherhood Lessons

This edition published by arrangement with Harlequin Books S.A.

For questions and comments about the quality of this book, please contact us at CustomerService@Harlequin.com.

Love Inspired
22 Adelaide St. West, 41st Floor
Toronto, Ontario M5H 4E3, Canada
www.LoveInspired.com

Printed in U.S.A.

Behold, I will do a new thing; now it shall spring forth; shall ye not know it? I will even make a way in the wilderness, and rivers in the desert.
—*Isaiah* 43:19

To my son, Asher. Your curiosity, determination and confidence never cease to amaze me! I can't wait to see what God has planned for your life. I love you.

Chapter One

If things had gone the way she'd planned, Merritt Lane would be on her honeymoon, vacationing on the island of Aruba right now. Instead, she was sitting on a dock in central Minnesota, her feet dangling in the cool lake, watching her four-year-old nieces play in the water.

Things had definitely not gone the way she had planned.

"Five more minutes," she called to Blair and Addison, trying to shift her thoughts away from her heartbreak. It had been two weeks since her fiancé had called everything off, but if she was honest with herself, she knew he had started to pull away months ago.

The twins' blond hair glowed in the sunshine, and their blue eyes turned to her in appeal.

"Ten more minutes, Auntie," Blair said with a big, convincing smile. "Please."

"Please," Addison added, her identical smile as bright as the noonday sun.

It was almost painful to see how much they looked like Merritt's sister, Reina. Just thinking about her sis-

ter brought up more unhappy memories that she had
to force aside.

"Okay," Merritt agreed, wondering how she would
ever say no to these two, even with six years of experience as a kindergarten teacher. "Ten minutes, but not
a minute more."

"Yay!" they both exclaimed and kicked their feet to
spin the floaties they were playing on.

Merritt allowed herself to smile as she moved aside
so the water didn't splash her. She had only arrived in
Minnesota yesterday, not even twenty-four hours ago.
The girls' nanny had called in desperate need for someone to come and stay with the girls while she went to
her daughter's aid after a car accident. Merritt had been
happy to leave South Carolina and the repercussions of
her canceled wedding. It was exactly what she'd needed
to start the healing process—if healing was possible.

She'd only been to Minnesota twice before—the
first time for her sister's wedding to Blair and Addison's
father, Knox Taylor, and the second time after the
twins had been born. But it had been almost five
years—and she hated to admit she hadn't seen the
girls since they were two weeks old. Thankfully, Blair
and Addison had not been shy when she arrived, and
Merritt's work as a kindergarten teacher had gone a
long way in helping her relate to the girls.

"Auntie," Addison said, turning her floatie to face
Merritt. "Is my daddy coming home?"

A bird twittered in a nearby tree and the waves
pushed gently against the dock posts as Merritt tried to
form an answer. She had no idea where Knox was currently working. Mrs. Masterson thought it was Japan,

but she had tried, in vain, for days to get ahold of him. That's why she had called Merritt.

"Of course he's coming home," Merritt told her niece.

"My mommy didn't come home," Blair said to Merritt, as if Merritt didn't know.

Reina, Merritt's half sister, had left the girls when they were three weeks old and had never come back.

What could Merritt say to Blair? She didn't really know the twins' father, Knox. His engagement to Reina had been a whirlwind affair, and there hadn't been any time to get to know him. She assumed he'd come back to the girls, but if Mrs. Masterson's occasional emails were any indication, Knox was only home a few times a year. There was no telling when he might show up again.

"I'm sure your daddy will be here as soon as he is able." Merritt stood and wiped her feet on one of the plush beach towels they had brought down to the lake. The Taylors' black Lab, Darby, stood at the same time, her tail wagging as she looked up at Merritt expectantly.

"Good." Addison kicked her feet, turning the floatie in the water. "I asked him to come home."

"You asked Daddy?" Blair stared at her sister.

"I called him and asked him to come home."

"When did you call him?" Merritt asked the little girl.

Addison shrugged.

"And you talked to your daddy?" Merritt was doubtful that the girl was telling the truth.

"I left a message." Addison spun on her floatie again, a giggle on her lips.

A boat sped by on the large lake, pulling a skier. Waves from the boat's wake lapped toward the girls. They laughed as the water pushed them up and then rolled them over the waves.

Messages seemed to be the only thing that people could leave for Knox. Merritt had tried to call him once, yesterday, when she'd arrived, but hadn't gotten through. His voice mail box had been full.

Where could he be?

Hopefully nothing serious had happened. If so, the girls would basically be orphaned. Their mother had given up full custody during her divorce almost five years ago and had all but disappeared. Merritt hadn't spoken to her for months, which was probably for the best, since they had never been close.

"Time's up," Merritt told the girls a few minutes later. "Let's get some lunch."

The girls grumbled but left the lake. After drying off, the three of them plodded toward the house, Darby following close behind.

It was a magnificent home, built on the shores of Tucker Lake, just outside Timber Falls, Minnesota. Merritt had been impressed upon seeing it for the first time when Reina had married Knox—and she was even more impressed now after her sister had done extensive renovations. In the middle of June, the lake, the house and the lush landscaping were picture-perfect. Everything looked magazine-ready, and Merritt was amazed she'd been offered the opportunity to spend time here with the girls. How much time, she wasn't sure—but at least until Knox could be reached. Mrs. Masterson thought it could be weeks—or months—before her daughter was well enough for her to return.

The house was cool as they stepped through the side door and into the lavish kitchen. Everything was top-quality, exactly how Reina had left it. And though Merritt and her sister were as different as night and day, she couldn't deny that Reina had an incredible sense of style.

While the girls climbed onto the counter stools and Darby went to her dish to lap up some water, Merritt went to the commercial-style refrigerator and opened the door. At the same moment, a man entered the kitchen, and the door almost hit him.

He grunted in surprise, and Merritt yelped, her heart rate escalating.

She slammed the door closed and came face-to-face with Knox Taylor.

"Daddy!" Addison called as she jumped down from the stool and ran toward her father.

Knox stood rooted in place, his gaze locked on Merritt, questions warring with the confusion and shock in his gaze. "What are you doing here?"

Merritt hadn't seen him in five years, and those years—though unkind for various reasons—had left him more handsome than she remembered. Which was no surprise. Her sister would never have married a man who wasn't extremely good-looking. Or rich. Or intriguing. Knox Taylor had been all those things, and more. He fit Reina's type—and for that reason alone, Merritt had not liked him.

But that didn't mean he didn't make her pulse race.

It took her a moment to pull herself together. "I came to watch the girls so Mrs. Masterson could be with her daughter."

Addison stopped in front of Knox and smiled up at him. "You came."

"Hello, sweetheart." Knox lifted his daughter and gave her a hug.

Blair watched from her place at the counter, making no move to join them.

Addison wrapped her arms around Knox's neck and looked like she wasn't about to let him go anytime soon. "You came, you came, you came."

Knox smiled as he hugged her back and glanced at his other daughter. "Hello, Blair-bear. Don't I get a hug?"

Blair frowned and shook her head. She jumped off the chair and ran out of the room—in the opposite direction as her sister.

Merritt stared after Blair, surprised at the way she had responded to her father's arrival. But could she blame the girl? Mrs. Masterson had said Knox had been gone for over eight weeks on this particular business trip.

With Addison still clinging to him, Knox turned his dark blue eyes to Merritt. He was tall and muscular—his very presence overwhelming the room. He was the kind of man who couldn't be overlooked—unlike Merritt, who had learned how to blend in from the moment she'd fainted from fear during her middle school Christmas concert.

"I'm sorry," he said, frowning in confusion at Merritt. "Why are you here?"

"Mrs. Masterson's daughter—" Merritt swallowed. Was he mad she had come? Surely he had no wish to see any of Reina's family ever again. Would he think she was overstepping? "She was in a car accident and is facing months of rehabilitation. Mrs. Masterson needed to get to her side and help with her grandchildren."

Knox continued to frown. "So she called you? Why didn't she call me?"

"She did, but she couldn't get through."

"And you were available to drop everything and come?" He studied her. "Wasn't there someone else who was closer?"

Merritt shrugged and shook her head. "I assume she asked everyone she could think of before she called me—including your parents." Surely Merritt hadn't been her first choice—not given the history between the Taylor and Lane families.

Knox finally nodded, his confusion turning to concern. "I hope it didn't inconvenience you."

What could she say? She'd been eager to accept the offer, to get away from the embarrassment of her canceled wedding and the reality that after six years of waiting for Brad Harrison to marry her, he had eloped with another woman. "Not in the least."

"And your husband—" Knox frowned again, apparently trying to remember Brad's name. "You were engaged last time you were here—right? Brian—or—"

"Brad." She could hardly say his name without a lump forming in her throat, threatening to make her cry.

"He's okay with you being here?"

Merritt swallowed hard. "Brad and I are not married." She tried to smile but failed miserably. "I don't know where he is, nor does he care where I am right now."

Knox had the decency to look away and nod in understanding.

She needed to change the subject. "Why are you here if you didn't get Mrs. Masterson's messages?"

It was Knox's turn to swallow as a look of deep sorrow and guilt washed over his face. He put his hand on Addison's back. "I came home when I heard Addy's message. It was the last one before my inbox was full." He looked back at Merritt, his eyes searching hers. "Is it ever too late to start over?"

Merritt shook her head, hoping and praying with all her heart that the answer was no.

Knox hadn't been home since Easter, and he hadn't planned to come back to the lake until closer to the Fourth of July. But the heartfelt message Addy had left on his phone had changed everything. Just the fact that she was old enough to call him and plead with him to come home had made Knox realize how quickly time was passing—and how much he had already missed.

The girls would be five years old at the beginning of August. How was it possible that it had been almost five years since his miserable marriage had ended and Reina had walked out on all of them for good? He'd run away for a long time, but he couldn't run forever.

Silence hung in the air as Merritt Lane stared at him, her soft brown eyes filled with so much pain and anguish, he had to look away. She didn't answer him but simply shook her head.

"Addy," Knox said as he tried to disentangle his daughter from around his neck. "I brought you and Blair some presents from Japan. They're in the brown bag by the door. Why don't you find her and show her what I brought?"

Addison's big blue eyes grew wide with interest and

excitement. She let him go and raced out of the kitchen, Darby on her heels. Addy's little pink flip-flops pattered as she went.

Knox stood to his full height and faced Merritt. He'd never thought he'd see her again. The two brief times they'd been together had been overshadowed by his wedding and then the birth of the twins. He didn't know much about her, other than her love for cooking and watching old movies. Those two facts had surprised him, since Reina had hated cooking and only watched reality television shows.

But what else did he know about Merritt Lane? She was Reina's half sister. And if they were anything alike, he knew all he needed to know.

"I feel like I need to catch up," Knox said as he crossed his arms and studied Merritt. She didn't look anything like Reina, which was easy enough to understand, since they had different moms. "What happened to Mrs. Masterson?"

"Her daughter was in a car accident." Merritt spoke slowly and deliberately, as if she was explaining something to a child—she was a teacher, wasn't she? "It was really serious, and her daughter is facing months of rehabilitation. Mrs. Masterson needed to leave as soon as possible to help with her grandchildren. She called me two days ago, and since I am currently—" She paused and looked down at her sandals. "Currently unemployed, I didn't have anything holding me back from coming." She looked up again, the dimples on either side of her mouth popping out as she pressed her lips together.

"Thank you for coming." It was the least he could say, wasn't it? She didn't have any obligation to help.

The only time the Lane family had reached out to him in the past five years was to send birthday cards to the girls with a bit of money tucked inside. Granted, he hadn't made any effort to contact them, but he wasn't even sure it would be welcomed.

"It's my pleasure," she said.

Knox moved away from Merritt and took a seat on the stool Blair had been occupying. He ran his hand over his face and through his hair, exhausted from the thirteen-hour flight from Tokyo to Minneapolis and then the two-hour drive from the airport to Tucker Lake. Even though it was noon here, it was the middle of the night in Japan, and he was still on Tokyo time.

He could hardly keep his eyes open.

"I suppose, now that you're here..." Merritt left the sentence dangling as she walked away from the refrigerator and went to stand near the door Addy had just exited. "You won't be needing me anymore. If I leave now, I could probably catch a flight to Charleston this evening."

Leave?

A surge of panic hit Knox at the idea of being alone with Addison and Blair. He'd never cared for them by himself. Mrs. Masterson had always been there to oversee the daily details. He hadn't shopped for them, cooked for them, cleaned for them—or been there when they learned to walk, potty train or ride a bike. Mrs. Masterson had been both a caregiver and a housekeeper in his absence. And he had paid her well for that service.

But if she was going to be gone for the summer— and Merritt was leaving—that would mean everything fell on Knox's shoulders. He could manage the cooking and cleaning—after all, he'd been a bachelor for most of his twenties—but he didn't know the first thing about childcare.

The panic mounted, and his mouth went dry. Could he ask Merritt to stay? He hardly knew her—had no idea if she'd even be interested—but he had to try. She was a schoolteacher, wasn't she? Maybe she'd be willing to stay on as the nanny.

He hadn't responded to her, and she was about to leave the kitchen, so he called out, "Do you have to leave?"

Merritt turned back to face him, her eyebrows tilting into a frown. "You want me to stay?"

The last thing he wanted to do was admit his inadequacies to Merritt, but she'd realize them sooner than later. "I have no idea what I'm doing with the girls. Mrs. Masterson moved into our house a few weeks before they were born, and I've never taken care of them without her help." He tried to hide the desperation and alarm from his voice. "If you're not free to stay, I completely understand. But—if you're looking for a temporary job, I'd be more than happy to pay you what I was paying her." And more, if necessary.

A quiet pause punctuated the room as Merritt studied him, her ever-present dimples appearing as she worried her bottom lip for a moment. "Just so I'm clear, what kind of work are you looking for me to do?"

"Childcare, some light housekeeping, cooking." He tried to smile.

"And will you be leaving again?"

He had called his boss and his administrative assistant and told them he would be working from home for the summer. As the chief toy engineer for Carbro Toys, he managed a team of designers and traveled the world to research toys from every continent on the globe. He also visited the manufacturing sites and worked with distribution channels, meeting with the head purchasers from several international retailers whenever they were about to kick off a new line of toys. Most of the work could be done remotely, and he wasn't scheduled for another trip until fall. "I don't have any immediate plans to leave."

Again, Merritt studied him, and he felt strangely vulnerable. There was something about her perceptive gaze that suggested she understood him far better than he understood himself. It was a bit unnerving.

"Don't you want to be involved in the care of your children and home?" Her question was so frank, and so direct, it took him by surprise. "The things we value the most should take the majority of our energy and attention."

If what she said was true, then it meant he valued his work far more than he valued his home and family. And that couldn't be true—or could it? If it was, then he needed to change things.

"Of course I want to be involved in the care of my children and home," he said defensively. "But I have to work, too. I've always made sure my daughters had the very best—even when I couldn't be here." Why did he feel like he had to explain himself? What did he have to prove to Merritt Lane?

"If you truly want to parent your daughters, then you don't need me."

Again, the panic mounted. He couldn't parent his daughters alone—at least, not yet. He didn't know the first thing about four-year-olds. Most dads were there on a day-to-day basis, learning as they went. He hadn't had the luxury.

Merritt looked like she was going to leave the kitchen again. He had to be honest with her—or she'd walk away.

"I don't know what I'm doing."

A gentle smile lifted Merritt's mouth, and her charming dimples appeared. "Then that's a different story entirely. Anyone can learn."

"Would you stay to help? I can pay you—"

"I don't want your money, Knox." Her smile disappeared, but her features were still soft. "But I will stay, if you really want me to, and help you learn what you need to know."

"You'd do that for me?" He hadn't thought Merritt would want to help him after what happened with her sister.

"I'd do it for all of you." She tilted her head toward the door where Addy had disappeared. "Those girls need you, more than anything else. More than a good nanny, presents or even this ginormous house. They need their daddy, and if you want to be there for them, I would love to help you do that."

Warmth filled his chest at her words. Her selflessness was unexpected and not at all what he had anticipated. It was yet one more thing that was nothing like Reina. He'd been so blind where his ex-wife was concerned—but that wasn't Merritt's fault. The only person he had to blame was himself. He couldn't assume that Merritt was like her sister. It wasn't fair to her.

Yet—he wouldn't let his guard down, either. He'd been hurt too deeply to trust anyone again—especially a Lane sister.

"So, you'll stay?" His voice was full of relief.

"I can stay, at least until the girls' birthday in early August. I will be looking for a new teaching position and will need to get back to South Carolina a couple weeks before school starts in mid-August."

That gave him almost two months for her to teach him everything he needed to know to be a good dad.

It felt like an impossible task.

"I suppose they'll be hungry for lunch." He stood, his body feeling weak and heavy with exhaustion.

"Why don't you get some sleep?" Again, she studied him with understanding. "I can manage tonight. You can get started first thing in the morning, after you've had some rest."

"Would you mind?" He was almost certain he could sleep for the next twenty-four hours and it still wouldn't be enough.

"I don't mind at all." She smiled, and the warmth of it wrapped around Knox like a hug, taking him by surprise. There was something so deeply kind about her.

He had a feeling Merritt Lane would continue to surprise him—first, with her unexpected appearance, and then with her offer to stay.

What other surprises did she have in store for him?

Chapter Two

A knock at the bedroom door tore Knox from his deep slumber. He opened one eye and glanced at the bedside clock. It wasn't even five o'clock in the morning yet.

With a groan, he rolled over to his stomach and closed his eyes again. Maybe he had just dreamed he heard something.

He was just about to doze off again when the knock sounded one more time.

"Knox," Merritt said through the solid oak door. "Wake up."

This time, Knox opened both of his eyes, adrenaline rushing through his body. What was she doing, waking him up in the middle of the night? Was something wrong? Were the girls hurt? Had someone broken in?

He jumped out of bed and went to the door. The shades were pulled down over the large windows facing the lake, but it was still dark outside.

Knox tore open the door and found Merritt standing in the hallway, dressed in a pair of shorts and a blouse, her hair pulled back in a ponytail. Darby stood next to her, eager anticipation in the wag of her black tail. Merritt didn't look like she was in a hurry—or too concerned.

When she saw him standing there in his pajamas, she looked down at the carpet. "Good morning."

"What's wrong?" he asked, wiping his hand over his eyes, trying to see straight. "Are the girls okay?"

"There's nothing wrong." She crossed her arms and then uncrossed them, a bit fidgety. "The girls will get up with the sun in about half an hour. It's a good idea to get up before them and get some of the chores rolling. Once they're up, it's harder to get things done."

Knox leaned against the door frame and stared at Merritt, his pulse slowing down. "There's no emergency?"

"Um." She frowned. "None that I know about."

"I thought—" He paused, not needing to tell her what he had thought. "Never mind." Suddenly, he felt exhausted again. All he wanted to do was climb back into bed. But the look on Merritt's face told him she was serious. "What kind of chores?"

"We should get a load of laundry going or it will start to stack up and we won't have any clean towels. We should also start breakfast—unless you want to feed the girls cereal or toaster pastry." She frowned and scrunched up her nose.

Apparently, cereal or pastry wasn't her idea of a good breakfast.

"Okay. Let me change." He moved away from the door and went to his bureau to grab one of his favorite T-shirts from college, a souvenir from a concert he had attended while studying at the University of Minnesota. Most of his suits and dress clothes were in his apartment in Minneapolis, but most of his casual clothes were here at the lake. When he wasn't traveling, he had split his time between the lake house and his apartment in downtown Minneapolis. Now, he was usually at the lake house if he was in Minnesota. It had always been a retreat and place of refuge—at least, until he'd married Reina.

Merritt had disappeared, so he went into the master bath and quickly brushed his teeth and ran his hand through his hair. He'd showered before bed last night, but he'd forgotten to shave. He didn't want to take the time now, suspecting that if he didn't show up downstairs in a minute or two, she'd be back to prod him along.

The smell of coffee drifted up to meet his nose as he walked down the back stairs into the kitchen. Merritt stood at the sink, filling a kettle with water. Darby stood outside the back door, staring at them through the glass panes. It was still dark out, but there was a hint of light tinging the sky.

"I hope the girls like oatmeal, though I doubt it." Merritt turned off the faucet and put the kettle on the stove. "Most children don't—but I do. What about you?"

"I don't mind it." He usually ate off a hotel menu, and they almost always offered some form of hot breakfast cereal. He went to the door and let Darby in. She went right to her food dish, which Merritt had already filled.

"I haven't been here long enough to know what the girls like or don't like," she continued as she went to the pantry and opened the door. "They ate the scrambled eggs and toast I made yesterday. I can always whip some up if they don't like oatmeal."

It was too early to think so deeply about food.

Knox went to the coffeepot and grabbed a mug from the cabinet nearby. The coffee was still brewing, but there was enough in the pot for half a cup. He removed the pot, and while he filled his mug, the stream of coffee trickled onto the warming plate below, sizzling and steaming.

"It's not ready." Merritt set down the container of oatmeal and came to his side. She took the pot out of his hand.

He let it go, since it was now empty. "I can't wait."

"Are you always this impatient?"

"Do you always follow all the rules?"

She smiled as she put the pot back onto the warming plate. "Yes. Always."

"Well," he chuckled. "I'm usually pretty patient. But it's early and I need some caffeine."

"That surprises me."

"What? That I need caffeine?"

"That you're patient."

"Really?" He frowned as he took a drink of the coffee. It was hot and scalded his tongue, but it was also exactly what he needed. When he was done drinking, he lowered the mug and looked at Merritt. "Why would you think I'm impatient? You hardly know me."

"That's true—but what I do know tells me quite a lot." She lifted the oatmeal container to study the instructions.

Knox set the mug down and crossed his arms as he leaned against the counter. What could she possibly know about him that would suggest he was impatient? "I'd love to know what led you to that assumption."

"Well." She lowered the oatmeal and studied him.

"I'd never heard of you before my sister called and told me that she was getting married to you, and that the wedding was in less than four weeks. That was the first thing that tipped me off."

The last thing Knox wanted to talk about was his wedding to Reina. "If you'll remember," he said quietly, "the twins were already on their way."

"Another clue about your personality." She didn't meet his gaze as she moved away from the counter and went to the dishwasher to start unloading. "You met my sister in Cancún on a vacation, and less than three weeks after she came home—in which time she didn't mention your name once—she found out she was expecting Addison and Blair." Merritt paused as she stacked the plates on the counter. "Clue number three."

Somehow, in the space of minutes, Merritt had dismantled his entire relationship with Reina. What she said was true. He'd met Reina on vacation and had spent almost every moment with her. He'd never had such a brief relationship with anyone before and promised himself he would never do anything like it again. She was a vivacious, gorgeous woman, and they had had a lot of fun together. She had completely beguiled him—and, knowing what he knew now, it was clear he wasn't the first man to fall for her charms. When he returned to Minneapolis, and she to Charleston, he hadn't known if he'd see her again.

When she called three weeks later and asked if she could fly out to Minneapolis for the weekend, he'd been thrilled, thinking that maybe there was something more to their relationship. But that's when she told him she was pregnant. Everything had happened at warp speed after that. Knox valued family and responsibility and knew that his grandfather, a minister, would be appalled if Knox didn't do the right thing. More than that, Knox *wanted* to do the right thing. So, Reina had quit her job as a personal trainer in Charleston and moved to Minneapolis a couple weeks later, and then they had celebrated with a small wedding at the lake four weeks after that. A couple days later, at a doctor's appointment, they'd learned they were having twins.

"Well," Knox said, pushing away from the counter, frustration and irritation making him feel the need to move. He couldn't hide the anger from his voice. "Things didn't really go as planned. If I had to do it all over again, things would have been a lot different." The whole experience had been almost surreal from beginning to end and so out of character for him, he still couldn't believe any of it had happened.

Except for the constant reminder of Addison and Blair.

Merritt stopped what she was doing and glanced up at him.

She had upset him, and he wasn't going to pretend otherwise. She'd passed judgment on him from one event in his life and had labeled him the worst sort of person.

He left the kitchen and went into the laundry room, where the clothes were already piling up. He tossed the dirty towels into the washing machine with more force than necessary and slammed the lid closed.

The truth was, he didn't blame Merritt for her assumptions. If he didn't know better and had observed that year of his life as an outsider, he would probably come to some pretty unflattering conclusions, too.

Hadn't he made some about her, just because of her sister?

Fifteen minutes later, after he folded the clothes from the dryer and let his temper cool off, he went back into the kitchen.

The girls had arrived, in their pajamas, and were sitting at the island drinking glasses of milk.

Knox was struck anew at how much they looked like Reina, especially as they aged.

Addison had her fingers in her mouth, playing with a tooth, but her face lit up and she said, "Daddy!"

Blair just frowned at him.

"Good morning," he said as he went to the island and hugged first Addison and then approached Blair. She didn't look at him, so he simply put his hand on her shoulder and gave it a gentle squeeze.

Merritt glanced at him as she stirred the oatmeal, an apology in her eyes. He shrugged and tried to act like their conversation hadn't bothered him.

"Who likes oatmeal?" Merritt asked.

Both the girls surprised him by raising their hands.

There was a lot he didn't know about his daughters.

While Merritt continued to stir the oatmeal, Darby started to make a strange sound deep in her throat.

"She's going to puke!" Blair said, her eyes wide with dread. "She ate too fast!"

"Out you go," Knox said as he rushed to the back door—but before he could open it, Darby threw up on the rug.

"Eww!" the girls cried.

Merritt scrunched up her face.

"I got it." Knox opened the door to let Darby out,

in case she felt the need to vomit again. He then went to the paper towel roll and pulled out several sheets.

"My tooth hurts," Addy said as she put her finger in her mouth again. Her eyes opened wide, and she pulled a little white tooth out. She threw the tooth on the counter, wails filling the air.

Knox frowned and stopped his trek over to the puke. He looked at Merritt with horror. "Is that normal?"

"Losing a tooth?" Merritt smiled and nodded. "She's almost five. It was bound to happen soon." She grabbed a paper towel and ran it under some water. "It's okay, Addy," she said.

Addy continued to cry as Knox bent down to clean up Darby's mess, while Merritt took care of the missing tooth.

Blair put her hands over her ears and scowled at all of them. "I can't take this anymore!"

"My oatmeal!" Merritt called as the scent of burned food met Knox's nose.

He tossed the dirty paper towels into the garbage can and then rushed over to the stove to remove the scorching pot from the burner.

At that moment, the smoke alarm went off, and Darby began to howl outside.

Knox's shoulders fell as he met Merritt's bewildered gaze.

What had they gotten themselves into?

The smoke alarm was unusually loud as Merritt held the wet paper towel against Addy's bleeding gum. "Here, sweetie," she said to the girl, "can you hold it?"

Tears streamed down Addy's face as she grabbed the paper towel from Merritt.

Knox took a kitchen towel and fanned the air in front of the smoke alarm. It finally stopped beeping.

"I know you're scared," Merritt said to Addy as she opened a window to let out the smoke, "but it's okay. It doesn't hurt anymore, does it?"

It took a moment for Addy to stop crying long enough for her to assess the situation. When she did, a huge grin filled her face, and she removed the paper towel to put her tongue where her tooth had just resided. "It *doesn't* hurt anymore!"

As a kindergarten teacher, Merritt had been there for several children who had lost their first tooth.

"Let me get you some salt water to swish around your mouth and the bleeding should stop."

Knox went to the cabinet and took out a glass before Merritt had the chance. He handed it to her, and she gave him a smile. "Thank you."

She filled the glass with water and table salt and then brought Addy to the sink and helped her swish.

The whole time, Knox watched in quiet fascination. She could see it in his eyes.

"I missed their first words and their first steps." He set the kitchen towel on the island counter. "But I was here to see her lose her first tooth."

"Pretty cool, isn't it?" Merritt asked him.

He nodded.

"It smells," Blair said, plugging her nose with one hand and pointing at the rug with the other.

"I should probably get the rug into the laundry room." Knox bent and lifted it up, folding it in half.

"Does Darby eat her food too fast all the time?" Merritt asked Blair.

The little girl stopped plugging her nose and nodded. "Mrs. Masterson always tells her to eat slower. She pukes *all* the time."

"Not *all* the time." Addy put her hand up to her mouth and giggled. "I sound funny," she said with a new lisp.

Blair giggled, too.

Merritt smiled.

A few minutes later, Knox returned to the kitchen. "I rinsed off the rug. I'll throw it into the wash when the towels are done." He went to the dishwasher, which Merritt had forgotten in all the busyness, and finished unloading. "How are you feeling, Addy?"

Addy grinned and showed off her missing bottom tooth.

"Don't forget to put your tooth under your pillow tonight," he said to her, "so the tooth fairy can find it."

The look of awe on Addy's face was priceless and warmed Merritt's heart.

Thirty minutes later, the kitchen was clean, everyone was fed and Darby was back to her old self.

Merritt had gone to her bedroom to change into a swimming suit. The girls had asked to swim in the lake again, and Knox had been eager to oblige. They were already in the water, but Merritt was taking her time, giving them a little space as a family.

She stood at the window, facing the lake, and watched Knox in the water with Addison and Blair. He was good with the girls, even if he was concerned that he didn't know what he was doing. Merritt was certain it was more fear than anything that drove his feelings. He looked like a natural with them, and they loved him. Yes, Blair was a little standoffish, but she was slowly warming.

He held Addison in his hands and spun her in a

large circle. Water splashed up in an arc from her feet, spraying Darby, who was on the dock, and creating a beautiful rainbow.

Merritt wrapped her arms around herself as she watched them. She really wasn't needed. Knox could do this on his own. But she didn't want to go back to her parents' house in South Carolina. She had moved out of her apartment in the beginning of May, in anticipation of marrying Brad and moving into his house after their wedding—but that hadn't happened. Not only was she homeless, but she was out of a job. Brad was the principal of the school she worked for, and she didn't think it would be smart to keep working for him.

If she didn't stay in Minnesota to help Knox, the summer ahead looked bleak.

But it wasn't just that. She had missed out on almost five years of the girls' lives. What kind of aunt was she? Granted, these were unusual circumstances—but that wasn't an excuse to be absent from Addison and Blair. Spending the summer with them would give her the opportunity to really get to know them and to make special memories.

Maybe, if Knox was willing, Merritt could also bring her parents into the picture. They didn't have any other grandchildren, and missing out on Addison's and Blair's lives was just as difficult for them as it was for Merritt. With the way things had ended between Knox and Reina, her parents hadn't been sure what— if anything—Knox would allow. Maybe spending the summer with him would help Merritt bridge that gap.

A text alert sounded from Merritt's phone, which was plugged in near her bed. She went to it and looked down. It was from her mom.

Merritt smiled. It always amazed her when her mom called or texted while she was thinking about her. It happened all the time.

The text read, How's it going?

It didn't pay to text her back. There was too much to tell. So Merritt unplugged the phone and pressed the call button.

"Hi, Mere," Mom said, her voice excited. "How's it going?"

"You'll never guess who showed up." Merritt walked back to the window and looked out at Knox and the girls again. "Knox is here."

"Knox?" Mom's voice was so high-pitched, Merritt moved the phone away from her ear for a second and laughed to herself. Mom was one of the most excitable people Merritt knew—and she loved her for it. Her mother felt everything—both good and bad—very deeply.

"He showed up yesterday afternoon, out of the blue."

"Does that mean you're coming home?"

"He asked me to stay."

There was a pause on the other end of the phone, then Mom said, "Do you think that's wise? We hardly know this man, except for what Reina told us. Do you trust him?"

"Mom." Merritt walked away from the window and paced across the guest bedroom. It was a huge room, with beautiful furniture. Everything spoke of wealth and opulence—exactly what Reina had planned when she redecorated, no doubt. "We have to remember that we only heard Reina's side of the story—and how often has she been trustworthy to give us the truth?"

"You're right." Mom sighed, and Merritt wondered

how many memories were floating through Mom's mind. As Reina's stepmom, things had not been easy for her. Reina had done everything she could to make Mom's life miserable—but Mom had tried her best to be the mother Reina needed. She'd come into Reina's life when Reina was two years old, but no matter how much Mom tried, Reina's feelings of abandonment and pain over her birth mother walking out on her had trumped anything Mom could accomplish. "Reina has always played the victim, so I shouldn't assume that the little she told us about Knox Taylor is true."

"From what I've seen, he's a good guy." Merritt paced back to the window and looked out again. Knox was pushing both girls around on their floaties, and they were all laughing. "He's a great dad—even if he's been pretty absent from their lives. The house is gorgeous, it appears that Mrs. Masterson is a wonderful caregiver and the girls have everything they need."

"Except their mother and father's attention."

"True." Merritt sighed. "Do you think it's a good idea for me to stay?"

"If it was me, I'd stay. I'd give pretty much anything to spend the summer with those girls. If your father and I hadn't invested so much money in the trip to Ireland, I would have gone to take care of them."

"I know." Mrs. Masterson had initially called and asked Merritt's parents to take care of the girls, but they had planned a once-in-a-lifetime tour of Ireland, and they would be leaving in two days.

"And with all that's happened in the past few weeks with Brad…" Mom let the sentence trail off.

"There isn't a better time."

"Exactly." Mom was quiet for a second and then said, "How long do you think you'll stay?"

"I'll plan on coming home right after the girls' birthday in August. I have a couple leads on a job in James Island, and I am hoping to have something secure well before then."

"You're going to live in James Island?" Mom's voice was full of hope.

Merritt had grown up in James Island, a suburb of Charleston, which was where her parents still lived. They had amazing schools, and Merritt would be blessed to get a job there. "That's what I hope."

"I'll be praying for you. For all of you."

"Thanks." Merritt knew that God had a plan for her life, even if that plan hurt sometimes. The knowledge that Brad had chosen someone over her—after six years of waiting for him—was the hardest thing to accept. Merritt had grown up in Reina's shadow, always coming in second-best in looks, popularity and friendships. It stung that she'd come in second-best in Brad's life, too.

Whenever Merritt achieved something to be proud of, Reina seemed to take the spotlight. It wasn't always a positive spotlight, either. Most of the time, Mom and Dad had to shift their focus off Merritt to deal with some sort of drama or trouble Reina found herself in.

When Merritt had gotten engaged to Brad six years ago, just a few weeks later, Reina had announced she was pregnant. Then she was getting married. The engagement party Mom and Dad had planned for Merritt had to be canceled because they were all going to Minnesota for Reina's wedding.

The engagement party was never rescheduled. And

when Merritt had finally convinced Brad to set a date the summer after, Reina had abandoned her husband and babies, and the family had been so embroiled in the mess, Merritt had decided to postpone her wedding. After that, Brad had one excuse or another to postpone it further.

"I should go," Merritt said to her mom. "Knox and the girls expect me to join them in the lake."

"Keep me posted. I'll try to check my phone as often as possible, but with the time change in Ireland, it might be difficult to connect."

"Have fun—and don't worry about us."

"I'll try not to. And if Knox is willing, let him know that Dad and I would love to plan a trip to Minnesota to see those girls again. We'll be back from Ireland in five weeks."

"I'll let him know."

"Love you, Mere."

"Love you, too, Mom." Merritt hung up the phone and put it on the dresser.

Part of her was excited at the prospect of spending the summer with the girls—but the other part was a little leery of Knox Taylor. She'd decided long ago what she thought about him, but everything she'd witnessed in the past twenty-four hours suggested that she had been wrong.

If he wasn't who Merritt thought he was, then who was he?

Chapter Three

Knox was out of breath as he left the water and lay down on his towel, which he'd left on the beach. The sunshine felt good against his bare chest.

"Daddy!" Blair called. "Again!"

"I need a little break," he called back, glancing at his daughters as they stood in the water, two identical blond-haired moppets, wet from splashing in the lake for the past thirty minutes.

"Let's build a sandcastle," Addy said to Blair.

"Okay." The girls left the water, and Knox sat up on his towel to watch them. They had brought their lake basket full of sand toys, and they dumped them onto the beach to start working.

June was Knox's favorite time of year at Tucker Lake. He loved everything about his vacation home, which had become a full-time residence for his daughters.

Merritt left the house and walked toward him. She was wearing a swimming suit with a modest cover-up and a large floppy hat. Her sunglasses hid her brown eyes, but they could not hide the deep dimples that came out to play when she smiled at him.

His breath caught at that smile. The first two times he'd met her, he'd been in over his head with Reina and hadn't noticed Merritt. Then, yesterday, when he'd come across her unexpectedly, he'd been too confused to notice. This morning, during their chaotic breakfast and her assumptions about his character, he'd been too distracted.

But right now, with nothing hindering him, he couldn't help but notice her.

She was a beautiful woman. Not gorgeous, like Reina—but lovely in her own quiet way. She looked like she could be just as comfortable attending a gala in an evening gown as she would be in an apron with finger paint staining her hands. Even if he didn't know she was a teacher, that's exactly what he would have guessed upon meeting her. She was patient, gentle and very kind. She had a way with his girls that even Mrs. Masterson lacked. They respected her but also treated her in a warm and affectionate manner.

"Another beautiful day," she said as she laid her beach towel on the sand a few feet away from him. "Does this ever get old?"

Knox grinned, forcing himself to let his thoughts rest. Merritt was his daughters' aunt. Nothing more. To even contemplate something different would be too complicated. "No, it doesn't get old—and the moment you think it might, it's autumn and everything changes."

"I bet the trees are beautiful here during the fall."

"Every season is beautiful." He pointed to a ridge on the opposite side of the lake, where a stand of white pine trees rose toward the sky. "In the winter, when the lake is frozen, and those trees over there are laden with snow, it's breathtaking."

"Have you lived here long?"

"I grew up on this lake. My parents rented a cabin every summer in the next bay over. There's a little resort with a handful of simple, two-room cabins. My mom was a fourth-grade teacher, so she had her summers off, and we would move out here for several months. My dad is an architect, and he drove into work every day in Timber Falls and then came out for the evenings."

"I didn't know your mom was a teacher."

"She was a really good teacher." He smiled at Merritt, realizing then how much she reminded him of his mom. "She retired a couple years ago. I think you'd like her."

"I probably would."

Warmth at the idea filled Knox, and he had to force himself to change the direction of his thoughts again. He would have been so much prouder introducing Merritt to his parents than he had been of Reina, especially under the circumstances.

"My older sister and I spent all day in the water, swimming, fishing and canoeing," he continued. "We used to catch turtles and have turtle races with the other kids who stayed at the resort for the summer." He drew his knee up and rested his elbow there as he looked out on the familiar lake, his thoughts years away. "Weekends were the best, when my dad would be there the whole time. My mom had special recipes she only made at the lake, and we would eat until we couldn't eat anymore."

"Is that why you bought this place?"

Knox glanced back at his home. It was a far cry from the two-room cabin he'd stayed in at the resort, but he loved it. "When we went out on the canoes, we would paddle past all these grand houses, and I told my sister that I would own one someday. I rent a modest apartment in Minneapolis, so when this house came up for sale about eight years ago, I thought it would be a good investment."

"Did you ever plan to live here full-time?"

"Eventually." He glanced at the girls, who were absorbed in their sandcastle. "But I had no idea things would turn out the way they did. I'm happy I had a home for them to grow up in, and I'm even happier that it's on this lake that meant so much to me when I was a kid."

"You're doing a great job, Knox."

His focus shifted to Merritt. She took off her sunglasses and smiled. Her eyes were so full of compassion and understanding, he had to swallow and look away. "It doesn't always feel that way."

"Feelings are rarely reliable." She chuckled. "I know a lot of kids their age, and I can tell you they are doing great. They're smart, well-mannered and genuinely happy."

Guilt weighed heavy on Knox as he thought about all the ways he was failing them.

But that was going to change. He'd already wasted enough time licking his wounds where Reina was concerned. It was time to pick up the pieces and get on with his life. He owed it to the girls—and to himself.

"Thanks." He adjusted his seat on the towel, uncomfortable with her compliments.

"Do your parents still live in Timber Falls?" She set her sunglasses aside and leaned back on her hands as she looked out at the lake.

He was thankful she changed the subject. "They moved to St. Louis a few years ago. My dad got a job offer they couldn't refuse—but they visit as often as they can. I talked to my mom this morning and found out that her and my dad are on a cruise right now. That's why Mrs. Masterson called you." He was happy that she had.

"Do you still have friends in Timber Falls?"

The town was about a twenty-minute drive from Tucker Lake and the closest town for shopping and school. The girls would need to be enrolled there in the fall. Something he hoped Mrs. Masterson had taken care of. He'd have to call her when he had a chance to ask.

"A few people, I suppose. I don't get there too often."

"I was thinking about taking the girls to church on Sunday—if that's okay with you."

Knox nodded. "They go with Mrs. Masterson to Timber Falls Community Church. From what I've heard, they have a lot of friends there."

Merritt shifted her gaze to Knox, her voice gentle. "Would you like to join us?"

It had been years since Knox had gone to church. After what had happened with Reina, he was embarrassed to attend. He wasn't proud of his choices, but if he knew anything about God and church, he'd still be welcomed. He just needed to take the first step. "I'd like that. I grew up going to church there. It would be nice to visit and see if I still know anyone."

"Good."

Merritt's smile did something funny to him again—filled him with pleasure. He liked making her happy. Liked seeing those dimples shining in his direction.

The girls left their sandcastle and came over to stand in front of Knox. Addy looked at Blair, her eyes full of uncertainty.

Blair stood there boldly, her hands on her hips.

"What would you like?" Knox asked his daughter.

"A playhouse."

"A playhouse?"

"One with real windows and doors and rooms." Blair watched him, her gaze unwavering.

Addy was a little timid as she stood to the side and back of her sister. But she also watched Knox's reaction.

"For our birthday," Blair continued.

"Where would we put a playhouse?" Knox asked, his mind already forming all sorts of possibilities. He'd studied consumer engineering at the University of Minnesota and had taken several courses in drafting and design. Without much trouble, he was already imagining different possibilities for a playhouse design.

"There." Blair pointed to a spot in the yard, closer to the house, under an ancient oak. It was a level area, with a great view from the house, so it would be easy to keep an eye on the girls from the kitchen.

"Building a playhouse is a lot of work," Knox told them.

"You could always buy a prefab playhouse," Merritt suggested.

"Where would the fun be in that?" he teased.

"Could it have a real fireplace?" Addy asked.

"And a kitchen sink?" Blair asked. "With real water?"

Knox shook his head. "No fire or water."

"A wise decision," Merritt chuckled.

Addy clapped her hands together. "Can we help you build it?"

"Hmm." Knox pressed his lips together as he thought about what it would take to build the girls a playhouse. He would still be working from home this summer, but he didn't have a lot to occupy his time. If there was ever a summer to build a playhouse for the girls, it would be this one. They were the perfect age for one, and though they were young, he was certain he could find something for them to help with. "I think that would be okay."

"Yay!" The girls jumped up and down, cheering loudly.

"How about we start working on the design tonight, and then when it's ready," Knox said, "we can take the design into Timber Falls and see how much it would cost for the materials."

"That sounds like a daunting project." Merritt looked a little skeptical. "Do you think you can have it finished by their birthday?"

"Seven weeks?" Knox laughed, puffing out his chest and lowering his voice for affect. "I could build a full-scale house in seven weeks."

Merritt rolled her eyes playfully.

"Can we have an upstairs and a downstairs?" Blair asked. "And two bedrooms and a living room—"

"We'll see." Knox didn't want to get her hopes too high.

"It sounds more impressive than the little cabin your family rented as a child," Merritt mused.

"I'll keep it simple."

"For some reason, I doubt it." Merritt laughed,

and he was surprised, all over again, at how well she seemed to know him.

The girls kept talking about their playhouse, and it was clear they had been thinking about it for a long time.

Knox loved a good project, especially one that involved designing and construction. It was the reason he'd gone into the toy business to begin with. As a boy, he had spent hours building his own toys and inventing new games. To do it as an adult, and get paid, had been his dream.

The summer now had a new purpose, and Knox couldn't wait to get started.

By the time they were ready to put the girls to bed, Merritt was exhausted. It was one thing to spend a day with fifteen kindergartners and then send them home for the evening—and another to spend an entire day with two preschoolers and not have the luxury of sending them off at three o'clock.

But they'd had a great day, full of sunshine, games and good food. Mrs. Masterson had left the kitchen well stocked, and Knox had made them hamburgers on the grill and fresh-cut French fries for supper.

"Daddy?" Addison asked as she got into her bed and pulled the covers up. "Will you pray for us?"

Knox had helped Merritt give the girls a bath and had patiently combed Addison's hair while Merritt had done the same for Blair. He stood between the girls' beds and gave Merritt a pleading look.

"I haven't prayed in a long time," he said.

Blair climbed into her bed, and Merritt reached down to pull up her covers. She stopped Merritt's hand when the covers got to her waist and pointed at the pony on her nightgown and said, "I don't want to cover Princess."

"Princess?"

"My pony. She can't breathe under the covers."

Knox hid his smile, but Merritt nodded, very serious. "I completely understand."

"Do you have your tooth?" Knox asked Addy.

Addy jumped up and lifted her pillow. The tooth was lying there. "Yep!"

"Don't forget to check and see if there's money there tomorrow morning." Knox helped tuck her back under her covers.

"I won't." Addy's face was so solemn, it was Merritt's turn to hide her smile.

"Well?" Blair said to Knox.

"Well, what?"

"Are you going to pray? Mrs. Masterson always prays."

Again, that panicked look came over Knox's face. Merritt couldn't help but feel bad for him.

"Could I pray again tonight?" Merritt asked the girls. "I've been wanting to thank God for sending me here."

"Okay." Addy nodded.

Merritt walked around Blair's bed and had to press past Knox to move between the girls.

He smelled good—really good—but she tried not to notice.

Instead, she knelt between the girls and took one of their hands in each of hers.

Knox stood behind her.

"Dear God," Merritt began. "Thank You so much for Addison and Blair—"

"And Daddy," Addison added on a whisper.

"And for their daddy," Merritt amended. "Thank You that we can all be here together. We ask that You bless Mrs. Masterson and her daughter and help her to get better fast."

"And we pray for Mommy," Blair said. "We want to meet her."

Merritt opened her eyes and found Blair pressing her eyelids closed tight. She glanced over her shoulder and caught Knox's gaze. It was hard to read his emotions as they played across his face.

"Please bless Reina," Merritt said, genuinely concerned for her sister. "And help her to be safe. Amen."

It was a simple prayer, but the girls were young, and it seemed to be enough.

"Amen," they both called out in unison.

"Amen," Knox said quietly behind her.

"Time for sleep." Merritt kissed each girl on the forehead and then stood and followed Knox out of their bedroom. She turned off the light, and a solar-powered night-light flipped on. "Good night, girls."

"Good night, Auntie," they both called back.

When Knox and Merritt were standing outside their bedroom, in the darkening hall, neither of them said anything for a moment. The sun had not yet set, and there was a riot of colors splayed across the sky, just outside the windows in the great room over the railing.

"Would you like to watch the sunset?" he asked quietly. "We have a great view of the western skyline from the patio."

Merritt had planned to pull out her laptop and look

for jobs—but she couldn't deny herself the pleasure of watching the sunset over the lake. How often did she get that opportunity?

"I'd love to."

"I'll start a fire in the fire pit." He let his gaze travel over her, and then he said, "You might want to grab a sweatshirt. It cools down quite a bit here at night."

She swallowed and nodded. It felt intimate standing in the hall with him—and the thought of spending the evening around a fire, watching the sunset, without the distraction of the girls, made her pulse tick a little harder. "Would you like some coffee or tea?"

His smile hitched up the corner of his mouth, and he nodded. "Some tea would be nice."

"Okay. I'll meet you outside."

He turned and walked down the main staircase and into the great room.

Merritt let out a long breath. She had to be careful. Knox was a good-looking man, possibly the most handsome guy she'd ever met. It would be easy to get her head turned by him. But there was too much at stake. She was healing from a breakup, but more than that, she had promised herself a long time ago that she would never date someone Reina had tossed aside. There had been more than one boyfriend who had come crying to Merritt over the years, but she knew that if she dated them, she'd only be second-best. To be interested in the man Reina had married would be unthinkable.

She pushed aside the thoughts and went to her bedroom to grab a cardigan. After she pulled it over her shoulders, she went to the kitchen. Long shadows slanted through the room, offering a peaceful glow. Darby was asleep on her bed near the laundry room, but she perked up upon seeing Merritt and followed her around the kitchen as she made the tea.

Just outside the back of the house, a large patio spread out toward the lake. A fire pit had been built into the patio and Knox was there, starting a fire. He wore a pair of khaki shorts and had pulled on a long-sleeve shirt over his T-shirt. His hair was tousled from wind and curled, just slightly, around his ears.

Merritt just stood for a moment, waiting for the tea-kettle to warm up, trying to imagine why Reina would give all this up. The house, the lake, the girls and Knox. What could possibly be better than this life? It was the very thing that Merritt had always dreamed about and had hoped to have with Brad. Yet it had stayed out of her reach. The pain of Brad's rejection was deep, but it wasn't as strong as she had thought it might be. Their engagement had been so long and so tumultuous— and he'd been so distant at the end—a part of her had known things wouldn't work out. Even if the final blow had been devastating.

With a sigh, she took the steaming kettle off the stove and put it on a tray she found tucked into a shelf. There was an array of teas to choose from, so she put out several and found the mugs and some local Wilson's honey in the pantry. She also found some lemon cookies, so she put those on a plate and then carried the tray out to the patio.

Knox stood from the fire pit and wiped his hands as he turned in her direction. The sky was full of color behind him, reflecting off the lake.

"Thanks," he said as she set the tray on the patio table. "This looks great."

They stood side by side as they made their tea.

Merritt tried not to notice when their arms brushed together. She was such a ninny. Knox was probably oblivious to her growing attraction—which was for the best. She needed to hide it.

There were some Adirondack chairs circling the fire pit. Merritt took a seat on one while Knox sat beside her on another.

A few fishing boats dotted the lake, their red and green night-lights bobbing up and down on the water. Darby had followed Merritt out, and she lay down near her feet, seemingly content to just be still.

"This is nice," Knox said as he leaned back in his chair. "I've never worked so hard in my life as I did today with those girls. I can't believe you do this for a living—and with more kids."

Merritt laughed. "It isn't easy, but I love it."

He studied her for a couple of seconds. "I have a feeling you're a great teacher."

She tried not to blush. "Thanks."

They sat in companionable silence for a couple minutes, and Merritt loved that she didn't feel obligated to fill the void.

"Can I ask what happened with Brad?" Knox's voice was tentative and gentle.

Merritt let out a sigh. She didn't want to talk about her ex-fiancé, but what was the point in avoiding it? "We were supposed to get married last week."

"What?" Knox almost knocked over his tea but saved it in time, only spilling a little on the arm of the chair. "Are you serious?"

"He called it off a week before that." Merritt licked her lips, which suddenly felt dry.

Knox squinted and seemed to be calculating something in his mind. "But you were engaged when you came for our wedding. That was six years ago. I thought you'd be married already."

Merritt was well aware of how long it had been. "We were supposed to get married the summer after we came here, but then Reina left and it didn't feel right to continue with our plans, so I postponed it. After that, I couldn't get Brad to agree to a date. He's the principal of the school I worked at, so he didn't want to get married during the school year. But each summer, something else came up. His two sisters had weddings on two consecutive summers, and he did a teacher's exchange program to Italy during a third." She swallowed. "Apparently, he met another school principal during his trip. She was from Georgia. He claims they were only friends at first." She tried not to let her anger tint her words. "They tried keeping it platonic for the past two years, but they could no longer deny their feelings for one another. They ran away together days after he broke off our engagement and, according to social media, are now married and on the honeymoon I was supposed to be on."

"Ouch. Did you have any idea?"

"Not really. I knew he had become distant the past few months, but I had no idea he was seeing another woman—or that it had been happening for so long. He didn't mention her to me once."

"I'm sorry, Merritt."

"It's not your fault."

"I know, but I'm sorry you had to go through that."

She lifted her tea bag out of her mug to set on the saucer. "It's still really fresh, but I'm happy to be here. It's been helpful for me to keep my mind occupied. I don't know what I'd do in Charleston right now. I gave up my apartment and was living with my parents."

He made a face, and she smiled.

"It wasn't so bad," she assured him. "I love my mom and dad—but it's a little weird moving back in when you're twenty-eight years old."

Knox's eyes were kind as he regarded her. "Brad made a huge mistake."

Butterflies filled Merritt's stomach at his words, but she tried to ignore them. "I appreciate that." What she wanted to say was that Reina had, too.

He looked away, toward the setting sun.

"What about you?" She didn't want to be the only one baring her soul tonight. It made her feel too vulnerable. "Any romances after Reina?"

"Nope." He shook his head, his voice decisive. "I'm done with all that."

Merritt frowned. "You're done with romance? For good?"

"It's not worth the heartache."

His words hit a raw place in her chest. "Maybe." But Merritt was a romantic. She couldn't imagine not wanting to fall in love again—regardless of the risk. "What if you could find the love of your life? Have a happy marriage? Do you really want to be alone for the rest of your life?"

"Do you really think it's possible to have that kind of a love story?" He studied her, the firelight reflecting in his eyes.

"I have to believe it's possible," she said quietly.

Knox sighed. "Then I guess I'll have to let you believe for me."

Their conversation shifted, but Merritt couldn't stop

thinking about what he'd said. She believed in true love, even if she'd never experienced it.

Was it possible that she was wrong?

Chapter Four

Knox wasn't excited about the direction of their conversation. Reina had not only hurt him, but she had made him rethink almost everything he knew about himself. Before meeting her, he had considered himself a smart, levelheaded kind of guy. But she had blindsided him. He should have been smarter, should have seen through the veneer to realize she was only using him and would dispose of him as soon as it wasn't fun anymore. He had always prided himself on being a good judge of character—so how had he missed all the red flags where Reina was concerned? Would he do it again? Fall head over heels in love, only to realize his mistake when it was too late?

It was safer to be jaded and cynical where love was concerned and to not open himself up to be hurt again.

And it was also safer to change the subject.

He readjusted his position in the Adirondack chair as the last sliver of sun dipped below the horizon and disappeared. "Did you say you were planning to look for another job tonight?"

Merritt held her tea mug in both her hands and nodded. "I was going to look online. School starts in about ten weeks in South Carolina."

"Are you planning to stay in the Charleston area?"

She shrugged. "I'm hoping to find a job in James Island, where I grew up. My parents would love to have me closer."

"Have you ever considered leaving South Carolina?"

She looked at him, questions in her beautiful brown eyes. He'd never noticed how brown they were before. In the flickering firelight, they almost looked like melted chocolate. "Why would I leave South Carolina?"

Knox glanced away from her, trying to take his mind off her eyes. "I don't know. I thought maybe you were adventurous, like your sister."

It was the wrong thing to say—and he knew it the moment the words left his lips.

Merritt stiffened and lifted her chin. "I'm nothing like Reina."

He opened his mouth to apologize, not sure if he had insulted her—or hurt her. "I'm sorry. I didn't mean to imply—"

"Reina has no interest in anything but herself," Merritt continued, seemingly unaware of Knox's apology. "She and I are complete opposites. I would give almost anything for all this." She motioned to the house, the lake, the kids' toys nearby—and then she paused as her hand pointed to him. Slowly, she lowered it and swallowed. "She was too self-absorbed to realize how blessed she was."

Knox studied Merritt, noting the heightened color in her cheeks, whether from the sunshine earlier in the day or from embarrassment now, he wasn't sure—but it made her look pretty.

"I love to travel and have fun," Merritt said, her voice a little quieter. "I love to be adventurous and spontaneous—I came here without giving it much thought—but, at the end of the day, all I really want is a place to put down some roots and start to build something that truly matters."

"And what is that?"

She regarded him, her eyes full of emotion. "A home. A family." She bit her bottom lip as she looked down at her tea. "A marriage—if you can believe that."

"I can believe that." It wasn't hard for Knox to imagine Merritt being a wife and mother. She seemed born for the roles. She was a natural with the girls—and, as far as a marriage went, she would make some guy really happy.

"You must think I'm strange," she said.

"Why?"

"Most women my age are focused on their careers, not even thinking about a home and family yet. Especially after being left at the altar."

"I don't think it's strange." He smiled. "I think it's refreshing." And endearing—though he wouldn't tell her that. He was surrounded by career-minded women at work. He had great respect for them, but he also respected a woman who wanted to put her focus and energy into raising a houseful of kids. "The world needs all kinds of women. And the great thing is that you can have both a career and a family. My mom is the most amazing woman I've ever known. She poured herself into both her students and her family." He paused, wondering if she'd appreciate what he had to say next. "You kind of remind me of her."

Merritt studied him for a moment, and then a bright smile tilted her lips.

"I hope you don't mind me saying that," he added quickly.

"Not when you just told me she's the most amazing woman you've ever known."

Heat climbed up Knox's neck, and he busied himself with taking a sip of his tea. He liked Merritt—a lot. More than he should. But he hadn't been in her company long enough to really know her—and given his past experience at reading Reina wrong, he wasn't ready to trust his instincts where Merritt was concerned. Maybe this was all a song and dance for him. He had thought Reina was near perfection, and he'd been all wrong.

Yes, Merritt was nothing like Reina—that was becoming more and more clear. But was it all an act? He wasn't naive. He knew his wealth and lifestyle were attractive—women had always been drawn to him because of it. Wasn't that one of Reina's reasons for pursuing him? Under Minnesota divorce law, she had been entitled to half of everything he owned. Thankfully, they'd settled out of court, and he'd recovered well.

But just because his pocketbook had recovered didn't mean his heart had fully healed.

Was Merritt playing him from a different angle?

He hated that he was so cynical, but he didn't know how to overcome the hard lessons he'd learned from his divorce.

"I should probably let you get to that job hunting," he said as he stood from his chair. He hadn't planned to leave her so soon—or in such an abrupt way. But he didn't trust himself. Every time he'd grown close to a woman the past five years, the same doubt and cynicism had reared their ugly heads. Would he ever trust himself—or someone else—again?

She looked up at him, confusion in her tilted brow. "I'm not in any hurry—at least tonight."

He had hardly touched his tea, and the fire was still blazing bright. The night was early, and the stars were just starting to poke through the twilight. It was one of his favorite times of day at the lake, but it hadn't been a good idea to put himself into such an intimate situation with Merritt. If he wasn't careful, he could fall for her, and he had a sinking feeling where that would leave him. On the surface, she represented everything that he had ever desired in a life companion—but was it more than skin-deep? How could he ever know? Some people were brilliant at hiding the truth until it was too late.

"I'm still trying to catch up on my sleep," he said as an excuse. "And if tomorrow is anything like today, I'm going to need all the rest I can get." He tried to make his voice sound light and pleasant, while inside, his thoughts and emotions were dark and uncertain.

Merritt started to rise, but he held up his hand. "Don't rush yourself on my account. Feel free to stay out here and enjoy your tea. There's a lot of life left in the fire." He picked up his tea mug. "Good night."

She slowly lowered herself into her chair again, more confusion in her eyes. "Good night."

He walked into the kitchen and closed the door, feeling like he was being chased by something.

The kitchen was dark, and Knox just stood for a minute looking out the window. Merritt slowly relaxed back into the chair and lifted the tea mug to her lips, staring out at the lake, deep in thought.

He wanted to believe she was as amazing as she appeared, but he couldn't trust himself to make that call. It would be easier to keep some space between them and not have to worry about his—or her—feelings.

The next day, Merritt found herself weeding one of the flower beds outside Knox's house. It was cooler than yesterday, and the sky was overcast. The flower bed held a profusion of yellow daffodils, purple, pink and white irises, and a few other green plants that had yet to bloom. She didn't mind weeding—actually enjoyed it. Pulling up unwanted weeds was therapeutic and left her feeling like she had accomplished something. She also loved the smell of dirt and the feeling of it beneath her fingers.

Knox and the girls were sitting at the table on the back patio, under the large umbrella with a pad of paper and a pencil. Merritt couldn't see them from where she was kneeling in the dirt, but she could hear them. They were busy making plans for the playhouse they would build together. Merritt had heard them discuss everything from a drawbridge to a princess tower, but each time one of the girls made an unreasonable suggestion, Knox brought them back around with a more sensible idea. His patience with them was remarkable.

Merritt wiped at the sweat on her brow with the back of her arm. Even though it was cooler than yesterday, it was still hot. A nice dip in the lake would be needed after she was done. She stood and stretched, then peeked around the corner of the house to see if they had made any real progress on the drawing.

Knox caught her eye. He looked amazing today, especially when he smiled. His face was freshly shaved, and his dark hair had just enough wave in it to make him look a little boyish—though the rest of him was all grown man. He wore a simple T-shirt and khaki shorts with a pair of flip-flops—but he could have easily been on the cover of a magazine with his good looks. Merritt felt frumpy compared to him—especially with the dirt on her knees and hands, sweat dripping down her temples and back.

"You don't have to do that," he said to her with that charming smile in place. "The lawn maintenance company will take care of it when they come later this week."

"I don't mind." She shrugged as she wiped her hands together, clumps of dirt falling near her feet. "I actually enjoy it."

"Come see what we made," Addy told Merritt, pointing at the piece of paper and jumping up and down in her excitement. "It's like a castle!"

"Is that why I heard you talking about a drawbridge and a tower?" Merritt asked as she walked across the patio to join them.

Blair puckered up her lips in disappointment. "Daddy said we couldn't have a tower."

Merritt looked over their shoulders at the drawing, her mouth slipping open in wonder.

It was a mini-replica of Knox's lake house—at least, that's what it looked like at first glance. It was only one story tall, but it had many of the same angles and features as the big house.

"What do you think?" he asked.

"I'm impressed." Merritt was surprised at how big it would be. Several adults could easily fit inside.

"I want it to grow with them." He used the eraser of

his pencil to remove a smudge from the page. "When they get older, they can use it for slumber parties, and I can easily modify it later on to make it a guest cottage."

"And see here?" Blair asked, pointing to one of the windows. "We're going to have real glass windows—*and* real lights."

"But no water," Addy said with a pout.

"This looks like a huge project," Merritt said, a little skeptical. "You still think you can finish it by their birthday?"

"Sure." Knox shrugged as he looked up at her, his eyes trailing to her dirty hands and knees for a second before saying, "This'll be easy."

Merritt wiped at her sweaty brow again, feeling more and more self-conscious. Last night had been so nice, sitting with him on the patio. But something had changed—quickly—and he'd left her all alone. She had racked her brain, trying to figure out what had gone wrong. He had told her she reminded him of his mom, and she had said she didn't mind him telling her that, because he'd just said his mom was the most amazing woman he knew. Had he been embarrassed? Had he thought she was fishing for another compliment?

Whatever it was, he had become uncomfortable with her and had been distant that morning while they'd fed the girls and did some of the chores. She wanted to ask him about it but didn't know him well enough to dive so deep.

"Hello?" A woman's voice sounded from the trees and bushes near the property line.

Merritt, Knox, Addison and Blair shifted their attention to the side yard, where a woman and young girl appeared.

"Hello!" the lady said, waving at them. "I don't mean to be nosy, but we saw you sitting out here and thought we'd stop by and introduce ourselves. We just arrived at our cabin this morning and will be here for the rest of the summer. We thought it would be neighborly to stop by and say hi."

The woman spoke quickly, her voice dripping with sweetness. She was stunning, in an old movie star kind of way, and could have easily been a stand-in for Audrey Hepburn. Her soft pink cropped pants and sleeveless white shirt were spotless. Her brown hair was turned up in a twist at the back of her head, and she wore big, white-rimmed sunglasses and white canvas shoes on her feet.

"I'm Penelope Duvall," she said as she walked onto the patio, the girl right beside her. "We're next door in that charming little cottage. I just purchased it a couple months ago but finally made it up here from Edina."

Merritt had seen the "cottage" next door, which could easily be described as a mansion.

"And this is my daughter, Veronica," Penelope said.

Veronica was a little cutout of her dazzling mother and looked like she hadn't played in the dirt or sand a day in her life. And if her mother could have stepped in for Audrey Hepburn, this little cherub could have easily played alongside Shirley Temple, with her head full of curls and her cute little sundress and black Mary Jane shoes.

Knox stood and extended his hand to Penelope. "I'm Knox Taylor," he said with a handsome smile. "And these are my daughters, Addison and Blair."

"Twins!" Penelope clapped her hands together. "Oh,

how darling they are, and right about my Veronica's age, too."

"We're almost five," Blair said, while Addy tucked behind her dad.

"I'm five and a half," Veronica said, tilting her head and lifting her chin in the air.

Nothing like Shirley Temple.

Merritt stood to the side, feeling more and more self-conscious of the dirt and sweat smeared over her body—and the old T-shirt and worn shorts she'd thrown on to work in the flower bed.

She would have liked nothing more than to excuse herself, but Knox glanced in her direction. "This is my—um—" He paused, and it was clear he didn't know how to introduce her.

"I'm Merritt Lane," she said. "I'm the girls' aunt, helping with childcare and housework this summer."

"Oh, how nice," Penelope said, the sweetness still dripping. "My nanny is unpacking Veronica's room right now." She looked at Knox. "They're lifesavers, aren't they? I have no idea how I'd survive being a single mom without Nanny Clara."

"Merritt isn't our nanny," Knox said to clarify. "She's the girls' aunt, and she's being kind enough to help this summer."

"You must come over for supper tomorrow," Penelope said to him. "I don't know anyone up north. Cabin life is so new to me, and you look like just the person to tell me everything I need to know."

Knox's smile was quick, but he didn't say anything.

"I've always wanted this kind of thing for Veronica," Penelope continued. "Nature is so appealing, isn't it?

There's nothing quite like roughing it to teach the important lessons in life."

Knox glanced at the house next door, and Merritt could almost read his thoughts. Even the two-room cabin he vacationed in as a child wouldn't be considered "roughing it" by most people's standards. The monstrosity of a house Penelope had purchased for her summer use surely had all the modern conveniences and comforts needed.

"How long have you lived here?" Penelope asked Knox.

"I grew up on Tucker Lake."

"So then, you're a local." Her eyebrows rose high, as if it was the last thing she'd expected to hear. "But you look so sophisticated."

"I don't know about sophisticated." He ran a hand over the back of his neck and grinned at her. "I spent my childhood summers at the local resort and bought this house about eight years ago."

"It's so beautiful," she said. "I'd love to see inside sometime. When you come tomorrow, don't expect anything fancy—yet. I have a local designer coming from Timber Falls to see what we can do with the place. If I'm going to live here three months out of the year, I must make changes."

Merritt stared at Penelope, recognizing several traits she shared with Reina. Beauty, class, style. And then Merritt turned her attention to Knox and watched his reaction to her. Was he just as taken with his new neighbor as he had been with Reina? Was this his type? If he had a type, Penelope would probably be it.

It occurred to Merritt that Reina had been the one to walk away from Knox—not the other way around.

If she hadn't walked away, would Knox still be married to her? Was he looking for a woman like Penelope? Someone to decorate his home and hang off his every word?

They'd make a stunning couple, that was certain.

Merritt paled in comparison to Penelope, and she felt herself fading into the background, like she had done so often in Reina's presence. It wasn't even a conscious decision, but one that was second nature to her. It was easier to remove herself from a situation than to be willfully overlooked.

No one seemed to notice as she stepped into the kitchen—no one except Darby, who looked up at her from her doggy bed with expectant brown eyes. Her tail started to wag, and Merritt stopped to pet behind her ears.

Penelope's laughter seeped through the walls and windows, and Merritt glanced outside.

Knox was laughing with her, his eyes shining bright.

It suddenly felt like a long summer ahead.

Chapter Five

Knox sat on the stool near his drafting table and smiled as he looked down at the floorplans he had created for the girls' playhouse. It had been years since he'd used the drafting table at the lake house, which had originally been a college graduation gift from his parents. It felt good to put it to use again. Too often, he used a computer program to generate his toy designs. But there was something special about a piece of drafting paper and a sharp pencil. To hear the graphite scratching against the paper fibers, watch a line materialize beneath the tip of the pencil and see a design come to life. This feeling was the reason he'd become a designer in the beginning.

But it wasn't fun to keep it to himself. He loved sharing his designs, especially to get feedback. He had never created something that wasn't made better by a quality critique. In the morning, he'd show the design to the girls, to see what they thought, but right now, they were asleep.

The floor outside his office creaked, and he glanced

up to see Merritt walking by, toward the stairs, probably heading to bed.

"Hey," he said to catch her attention.

She stopped and took a step back to look into his office, her eyes wide and curious.

"Do you mind taking a look at something and giving me your opinion?" he asked.

With a nod, Merritt entered his office.

It wasn't a big room, but it was one of his favorites in the house. It looked out the side, toward the wooded part of his property. He'd opened a window to let in the cool night air, and just outside, the crickets were chirping while an owl hooted in the distance. It was dark and he couldn't see anything beyond the house.

"What would you like me to look at?" Merritt asked.

Her hair was pulled back in a loose ponytail, and she was wearing a pair of jean shorts and an oversize Charleston Southern University sweatshirt. He hadn't seen much of her that afternoon or evening, other than a brief conversation here and there. She'd disappeared when Penelope Duvall had shown up, and it had taken Knox almost an hour to politely ask his new neighbor to leave. Merritt had made some tacos and left everything out for him and the girls, but she hadn't joined them for supper.

Later, she'd come back to the kitchen, her hair wet from the shower, wearing the clean outfit she had on now. She had smelled amazing as she silently cleaned up, then took the girls out for a walk—one she didn't invite him to join.

After putting the girls to bed, she'd disappeared again, and this time, he caught sight of her in the great room, with her laptop open. He had assumed she was looking for a job, and he hadn't wanted to bother her, so he'd come into his office to work on the design.

But now, as she stood before him, he couldn't deny that he had been disappointed in how little they'd interacted that day. Was she giving him space because of how he'd treated her on the patio last night? Or maybe it was because of how distant he'd been to her that morning. Either way, she probably hadn't felt welcome in his home, and the only person he had to blame was himself.

It would be a long summer if he couldn't find a way to coexist with her without doubting her every move and intention.

He stood up from the stool and moved aside so she could see his design. "I was wondering if you'd take a look at the playhouse and let me know what you think."

She moved closer to him—close enough for him to smell the shampoo she used. He hadn't been close to a woman in a long time, and it did strange things to his pulse.

As she looked over his design, he couldn't take his eyes off her side profile. Her dimples were definitely her most striking feature—but her high cheekbones and the curve of her lips were equally as captivating.

"This is amazing," she said as she turned—and found him studying her.

There was something that drew him to her. Whether it was her quiet confidence, her gentle personality or her bright optimism, he wasn't sure. Maybe it was a mixture of all those things. He wanted to believe it wasn't an act—and was beginning to think the reason he was so leery of her was because she was authentic, and that scared him more than anything. If she was as amazing as she appeared, his heart was in trouble.

Their gazes collided, and she grew still, watching him.

"You like it?" he asked softly.

"I—I do," she said, tearing her gaze away from him. "But don't you think it's a bit too much to handle on your own?"

Even though she had looked away from him, he was still watching her. How had he not noticed how thick her hair was before, or how long her eyelashes?

"I know a few construction companies in Timber Falls I plan to call," he said. "I'm not worried about the project size—I'm just wondering if there's anything I need to change or add. What do you think?"

She continued to study the design for a minute, and then she shook her head. "It's perfect, Knox. I can't think of anything it's missing."

"Great." He was surprised at how good it felt to hear her praise his design. His chest felt warm with her approval. "I need to finish a few things, and then I'm going to take it to a lumberyard and get the supplies. I'm hoping to start the project by the beginning of next week." On instinct, he took her hand and said, "Come see where I want to put it."

She looked down at her small hand, wrapped inside his, a stunned expression in her eyes.

He realized what he had done and immediately dropped her hand. "Sorry."

"It's okay," she said quietly.

"Do you want to see where I plan to put it?"

"Sure."

He led her out of the office, down the hall and toward the kitchen. There, he turned on the outdoor lights, which flooded the backyard.

Darby looked up from her bed and rose to follow them.

"I like where the girls suggested we put it," he said, "but I thought of an even better spot." He slipped on his flip-flops and she did the same, then he opened the back door and let her pass through before him, Darby close on her heels.

They walked across the patio and turned the corner to head toward the wooded area. It was darker on this side of the house, with just the moon and stars for a night-light.

"Where are you taking me?" she asked quietly.

"It's not much farther."

The trees on this side of the house were so dense, he couldn't see his neighbor on the other side. Tall, thick white pines stood here, making the ground soft from their needles, which fell each autumn. A small clearing, close to the edge, would be the perfect place for the playhouse, which would one day be a guesthouse.

"There are only a few native stands of white pine trees left in Minnesota," Knox explained to Merritt. "When the lumber barons came through here in the early part of the twentieth century, they decimated most of the virgin pine. This piece of property was protected because one of those lumber barons, a man named Noah Asher, had fallen in love with Tucker Lake and put up a small cabin in this very spot. He wouldn't let them log any of these trees and would often come out here, all alone. He lived in a stunning mansion in Timber Falls, but out here, his cabin was nothing more

than a shack. He said the simplicity of the building reminded him of his humble beginnings.

"Sadly, when he passed away, his family parceled
off the land and sold it to the people who eventually
built the magnificent homes on this shoreline—but
they all honored his memory by leaving as many trees
here as possible."

"What an incredible story," Merritt breathed as she
followed him into the clearing. Their feet didn't make
a sound on the soft needles. "And it's pretty cool that
you know it."

"My mom loves history. She did a lot of research
on the Asher family because of her own love for this
lake. There's actually a picture of that original cabin
in my office. It was taken before they tore it down. My
mom found it at the local historical society and had a
copy made for me."

"I love history, too. Visiting historic sites and mu-
seums is one of my favorite things to do." Merritt indicated the clearing. "And that cabin was right here?"

He nodded as his eye caught sight of several fire-
flies floating in and among the tree trunks.

"Why did they tear it down?"

"It had become dangerous. The roof was rotten, and
the foundation had crumbled. I wish someone would
have tried to restore it, but the next best thing is to
build another structure on top of it that can bring other
people joy."

"Is this where you want to put the girls' playhouse?"

"That's what I was thinking, but I wanted another
opinion. It's close enough to the house, but there's still
some privacy here for when they grow a little older."

He waited to hear her thoughts. He didn't know why, but her opinion mattered a lot more than it should.

Merritt slowly walked around the clearing, her hands in the front pocket of her sweatshirt, as Darby followed her. She loved this place and felt a connection to it that surprised her. Just like his mom, she loved history and was already wondering when she might have a chance to see the picture in his office and stop by the historical society to learn more about the lumber baron Noah Asher.

"I think this is an amazing spot to put the playhouse." She pointed toward the main house, where she could see his office through the window, and knew that the other windows, which were dark, looked into the formal dining room. "And you could still keep an eye on the girls from inside."

Her gaze was captured by a firefly as it floated up toward the treetops overhead. The majestic pines were swaying gently in the wind, but it was the spectacular view of the stars beyond them that made her catch her breath. They were brilliant against the backdrop of inky blackness.

"I can see why Noah Asher liked to come here," she said softly. "I'd want to be here all the time. I could just lie here and watch the stars for hours. When you finish the playhouse, I'll come here and look up at that sky all night."

"Why wait?" he asked, just as quietly, as he lay down on the soft bed of needles. He stared up at the sky, a half smile on his face while Darby joined him.

Merritt stood for a moment, at first surprised but then delighted by his spontaneity. How many men would just lie down on a bed of pine needles to look up at the stars? It was something she would do without hesitation by herself, or with her kindergarten students, but it wasn't something she might have pictured Knox Taylor doing.

Without another thought, she lay down on the ground beside him, smiling at the pure enjoyment she felt.

The needles were thick and almost felt like a mattress as she lay on them. Her gaze wandered past the treetops to the stars, and her mouth slipped open in wonder. "I've never seen anything like it."

Her hand brushed against his, and the contact set the butterflies dancing in her stomach. Her first instinct was to pull her hand away—but she left it there, wondering what he might do.

He didn't move his hand away, either, and she recalled the way it had felt when he'd taken it in his before they'd left his office. His strength was evident, but it was his gentleness that had surprised her.

"I'm happy you're here, Merritt." His voice was low and tender, as if he didn't want to disturb the moment with too much noise.

"I am, too," she said, just as quietly.

"We didn't have a chance to get to know one another very well...before."

Her mind filled with all the memories of the times they'd been together—before, as he'd put it. Those experiences had been overshadowed by Reina. Would he ever think of Merritt without thinking of Reina at the same time?

She moved her hand away from him, trying to keep the years of pain and frustration out of her voice. "I wish you would stop thinking about Reina every time you think about me."

Knox lifted himself up and leaned on his elbow as he looked down at her, surprise and compassion stirring within his gaze.

She felt vulnerable under his attention. "You do, don't you?" she asked. "You've been comparing me to her every minute I've been here."

He didn't say anything—but what could he say? She knew it was true.

"I'm not my sister." She also rose up and leaned on her elbow, facing him. "I'm nothing like her. I've spent my entire life living in her shadow—and I don't want to live there anymore. I want you to know me for who *I* am and not who she is." She couldn't hide the longing in her voice. "Can't you try to imagine what it would have been like if you had met me without knowing her first?"

He studied her in the moonlight, and she wished she knew what he was thinking. There was sadness in his gaze. Finally, he nodded. "Okay, but only if you get to know me for who I am and not for the mistakes I made almost six years ago."

His request hit the center of her heart. He didn't wish to be known for his past, and neither did she. Did that mean they might start over and become friends?

She'd be lying to herself if she said she didn't wish for more. Her attraction to him was undeniable. Had Reina not found him first, Merritt might have harbored a wish for something deeper.

But even as she had the thought, she knew it wasn't true. Knox was nothing like the other men Merritt had dated. She had intentionally chosen men who were complete opposites of the ones Reina liked. If Reina went for a handsome, athletic, outgoing, popular kind of guy, Merritt had looked for the opposite—someone like Brad. He had been academic, pleasant to look at but not terribly handsome, well-liked, but definitely not someone who stood out in a crowd. He'd been reliable and predictable—yet, where had that gotten her? Jilted at the altar.

It suddenly left Merritt wondering what kind of a man she would have looked for had Reina not been her sister. Was Brad really the kind of man she would have chosen?

Or would she have looked for someone more like Knox?

"Do you think we can start over, Merritt?" Knox asked, tearing her thoughts away from the rabbit trail she'd just gone down. "Wipe the slate clean and get to know one another without all the past baggage?"

She nodded, eager to give it a try. "I think we can."

He smiled.

The lighter tone in their voices made Darby look up at them while she wagged her tail.

They lay on the ground to look at the stars again, but as they did, Merritt couldn't help but wonder how smart it was to let her guard down where Knox was concerned. He made her heart pump hard and her stomach turn with butterflies. Neither of those things was good for a simple, platonic friendship. If left unchecked, it could lead her to feelings she would eventually regret. Because the truth was, he *had* been married to Reina. Merritt could try to ignore that fact, could put it aside to get to know him. She could even accept that maybe he wasn't like all the other men Reina had dated. But, at the end of the day, Merritt could never live with the knowledge that if something developed between them, she would be his second choice. He hadn't been the one to initiate the divorce with her sister—Reina had walked away. That meant that, given the choice, Knox would still be married to her.

Merritt would always be in second place. And she could never live in second place to Reina. Never. No matter how much she liked Knox, no matter how much he might like her, the only thing that could ever reside between them was friendship.

In August, when she left Tucker Lake to return to James Island, the only thing she could take with her was the memory of this summer together.

But what she was afraid she might be taking was a broken heart.

Chapter Six

"Are we going to Veronica's house yet?" Blair asked Knox for the tenth time that afternoon.

"Yes," he said. "We're leaving as soon as Merritt and Addy get back from the store."

"Let's go without them," Blair begged. She'd been wanting to go next door since she'd woken up that morning. The lure of a new friend was too much for her to bear.

"That would be rude," Knox told his daughter as he closed his laptop and turned on his stool to look at her. He'd been working on a schedule for their playhouse project and making calls that morning trying to find an excavator, a cement company and an electrician. He'd need to line them all up now if he had any hope of getting the project finished by early August. Even then, he'd found it difficult to locate people who had openings in their summer schedule to stop by and give him estimates—let alone commit to working on the project. Most companies were booked for the summer months already.

The garage door opened, and Knox glanced outside. "It looks like they're back."

"Yay!" Blair called out as she ran from the office, toward the garage entrance.

When Knox had asked Penelope what they could bring for supper that evening, she had said they didn't need to bring anything. But Knox had insisted, so she had told him to bring some beverages. There wasn't much in the house, so Merritt had volunteered to run into town to grab a few things.

"Sorry we're so late," Merritt said to Knox as she came into the foyer, her hands full of grocery bags. "I thought it would be fun to make a few of my family's favorite dishes to share with the girls and ended up buying more food than I had planned."

"Here," Knox said as he took a the bags. "Let me help."

"Thank you." She also held a pretty bouquet of flowers. "I thought it would be a nice gesture to take flowers to Penelope as a hostess gift and a welcome to the neighborhood."

"That was really thoughtful." Knox smiled, appreciating Merritt's concern and consideration for others. "And the girls will love trying some of your family's favorite foods." He was looking forward to it, too. He knew very little about the Lane family. Merritt had spoken more about them in the three days she'd been at his home than Reina had in the year she'd lived with him. It was clear that Merritt's parents meant more to her than they had to her sister.

He checked his thoughts, reminding himself that he wasn't going to compare them anymore.

"Can we go?" Blair asked in a whiny tone.

"After we put away the groceries," Knox told his impatient daughter. "Go and see if there's anything else that needs to come in from the car."

Blair did as she was told, and soon all the groceries had been brought in and put away.

Merritt found a vase and arranged the fresh-cut flowers while Knox put together a basket of beverages to take next door.

They fed Darby, let her out one more time and then the four of them trekked across the side yard to enter the Duvalls' property.

Knox had never been in the house next door. The previous owners had rarely been there to visit while he was at home, and they'd been several years older than him. Other than a neighborly greeting once in a while, they'd never really spoken.

He could tell things would be a lot different with Penelope Duvall next door.

"Yoo-hoo!" she called out from the back patio of her home. "Welcome, welcome!"

Knox braced himself for her attention and gregarious personality. She'd been exhausting yesterday when she'd stopped by, and he hoped she'd be a little more relaxed in her own space today.

What he wasn't prepared for was finding her sunbathing in a two-piece swimming suit.

She wore a large, floppy hat and a pair of oversize sunglasses. When she stood up to greet him, he had to look away, since her bikini wasn't as modest as he would have liked with his daughters present.

"Oh, would you look at the time," she said, though she had no watch or clock to glance at. "I wasn't planning to get caught sunbathing when I had guests coming. How silly of me."

Knox glanced at Merritt, trying to find something to look at besides Penelope.

His gaze caught on the bouquet of flowers, and he took it from Merritt. "We've brought you some flowers. Can I go inside and set them down?"

"You brought me flowers?" Penelope had the decency to put on a swimsuit cover-up, though it was sheer and practically see-through. At least it hinted at modesty. "You shouldn't have, Knox."

"It was Merritt's idea," he said, hoping Penelope didn't take the gift the wrong way.

"Oh, Merritt." Penelope took the flowers and appeared to notice Merritt for the first time since their arrival. Her smile fell. "I didn't expect to see you this evening. I assumed Knox would give you the night off."

Merritt glanced at Knox, her cheeks turning pink. She opened her mouth to respond, but Penelope interrupted her.

"I gave my nanny the night off." She looked at Knox, her lips puckering into a pout. "I thought it would be more intimate if it was just the two of us and the girls."

Knox took a step closer to Merritt, wanting to both defend her from Penelope's assumptions and send Penelope the message that he had no intention of making this an intimate affair.

"Merritt is not my nanny," he said, "and I thought this would be a friendly barbecue, nothing more. If there's been some sort of misunderstanding, we can reschedule for a different time when you're more prepared for all of us."

"Oh, goodness, Knox." Penelope laughed as she sidled up beside him and put her hand on his forearm. "Everything's just fine. We'll laugh at this little misunderstanding in the years to come, I'm sure." She looked at Merritt, her smile wide. "Of course Merritt is welcome to stay, and I hope she does." She glanced from Merritt to Knox, her smile falling and her eyebrows rising high. "Unless I completely misunderstood and you and Merritt are a couple."

Both Knox and Merritt shook their heads, Merritt a little more adamant than Knox.

"I'm just here to help for the summer," Merritt said. "Nothing more."

Penelope studied them for another moment before she said, "Good."

Addison and Blair quickly found Veronica, who was lying on a lounge chair in her own swimming suit. A small, blow-up pool had been set up, and the girls asked if they could go swimming. Since they had their suits on under their dresses, Knox agreed.

"How about I go on up and change into something more comfortable," Penelope said. "My cook has been working on our meal all day." She took the basket of drinks they had brought and said, "I'll drop this off with her and she'll put everything on ice, then bring you two out a couple of glasses."

"You have a cook?" Merritt asked—and then pressed her lips together, as if the question had slipped past without thought.

"Of course—don't you?" Penelope stared at Merritt, her eyes open wide with surprise.

Merritt just shook her head.

Penelope smiled and then motioned to the girls. "Do you mind keeping an eye on Veronica, Merritt? Since you have so much experience babysitting. You are a kindergarten teacher, aren't you?"

"I'm a teacher," Merritt said through a forced smile. "Not a babysitter."

"Isn't it the same thing?" Penelope laughed at her own joke as she left the patio and went inside.

Merritt turned to Knox, several emotions in her gaze as she said, "I think I'll go back to your house, if you don't mind. It's clear I wasn't expected."

Alarm rang inside Knox, and he shook his head. "Please don't go. I really don't want to be alone with her." And, the truth was, he didn't want to see Merritt leave, because he'd been looking forward to spending the evening in her company. What he really wanted was to be at his own house, without Penelope, so he could have Merritt all to himself. But it was too late to back out now.

"I'm sorry, Knox," she said. "But I don't think she likes me, and it will be uncomfortable to stay."

"Please," he asked, taking a step closer to her. "Will you think about staying for me?"

She looked up at him, her brown eyes filled with a dozen questions, but she must have seen something in his gaze that made her want to agree, because she finally nodded. "Okay, but can we make it an early evening? I don't know how much of her I can handle."

"Of course we can make it an early evening." He hoped they could leave soon enough to allow him and her to maybe sit out on his own patio, like they had done the first evening, to get to know one another a little better. It was all he had thought about since they'd agreed to put the past behind them and start over the night before.

* * *

"I know," Penelope said a couple hours later as she pushed aside her dessert plate, which she'd hardly touched. "Why don't we all plan a day on the lake tomorrow?"

Merritt looked at Knox to see what he thought of the idea. She was already forming an excuse to avoid spending more time in Penelope's company and wondered how Knox would handle the situation. All throughout the meal, he'd been kind and polite, and he appeared to be experienced with a woman like Penelope, who made her intentions toward him plain.

"I can take out my speedboat," Penelope continued. "We can pull the girls on the inner tube, and I'd love to try my hand at waterskiing again. I used to be really good at it in high school."

"Thanks for the invitation," Knox said, "but I have a full day planned for the girls tomorrow."

He did? If he and the girls were busy, what would she do to occupy her time? Maybe she'd go into Timber Falls and check out the historical society or use the time to do a little more job searching. She'd found a few promising positions the night before but needed to work on her résumé and fill out the applications online.

Penelope pouted. "Can't you change your plans?"

"I don't think so." He shook his head. "I'm sorry."

The girls had been excused and were inside playing with Veronica's new dolls. It left Knox, Merritt and Penelope outside on the patio, under the umbrella. The sun was low on the horizon, and the lake traffic had quieted to a low hum.

Merritt hoped they could excuse themselves soon.

"Then I'm claiming the next day," Penelope said,

wagging her well-manicured finger at him. "You can't say no to me twice."

Merritt glanced at Knox, wishing she knew what he was thinking. He hid his feelings about Penelope well. Did he like her playful, flirtatious personality? Or was it just as annoying to him as it was to Merritt?

"Unfortunately, I have a big project I'm working on," Knox said. "I don't know how much time I'll have to enjoy the lake this summer."

"Well, that sounds boring." Penelope's voice was suddenly dry. "What's the point of living on a lake if you don't plan to use it?"

"I'm sure Merritt and the girls will get a lot of lake time." Knox smiled at Merritt. "But I need to work hard if I want to get the playhouse finished for the girls by their birthday."

"You're building them a playhouse? How sweet." Penelope took a sip of her drink. "When is their birthday party? I'll be sure to pencil it into my calendar."

"We haven't chosen which day to celebrate," Knox said, shrugging in a noncommittal way.

"Be sure to tell me," Penelope said as she reached over to fill Knox's glass again.

He put his hand over the top and shook his head. "I think it's about time we get back home."

Penelope started to protest, but both Merritt and Knox rose as one. Merritt was relieved the evening was coming to an end.

"I'll run in and get the girls," Merritt offered.

"I've got them." Knox moved away from the table and toward the house before Merritt could take a step.

When he was inside, it was just Merritt and Penelope on the patio.

Penelope's entire demeanor changed. She crossed her arms and looked Merritt over from head to toe.

"If the rumors I've heard are true," Penelope said slowly, a sly smile on her face, her voice changing, "Knox is quite the catch."

Merritt blinked several times before she opened her mouth to respond, but Penelope wasn't finished.

"He's wealthy, handsome and single. I've spoken to a couple of neighbors, and they all told me about Knox's first wife." Penelope lifted one perfectly sculpted eyebrow. "It sounds like she was pretty spoiled and wasn't happy living out here in the sticks. But that's where the two of us are different. I'm ready for some peace and quiet, and lake life suits me just fine."

"It sounds like you've done some homework."

"And why wouldn't I?" Penelope played with the gold bracelets on her wrist. "Knox is the most eligible bachelor in the area. I needed to know if I fit the description of the woman he's looking for."

"From what I can tell, he regrets marrying his first wife." Merritt wasn't ready to talk about her sister. "Maybe he's looking for the complete opposite."

"Someone like you?" Penelope laughed—for an uncomfortably long time.

Merritt lifted her chin, her suspicions about Penelope being confirmed. "It doesn't really matter, does it? I have no interest in Knox."

"Good." She stopped laughing and became serious again. "Because he'd never go for someone like you. You're much too— Oh, what's the word? Simple? Plain?" She lifted one shoulder. "He's sophisticated and out of your league. I would hate to see you get hurt. Besides, I would like us to be friends, and we couldn't be if you harbored any unrealistic feelings toward him."

Merritt was at a loss for words. There was no possible way she and Penelope could ever be friends. They were as different as two people could be, and beyond their close living proximity, they had nothing in common. She had no wish to stay and play the game with Penelope, so she motioned toward Knox's house. "Please let Knox know I've already left."

"Of course, dear." Penelope's smile was almost feline. "I'll make sure he finds his way back home… eventually."

It took all Merritt's willpower to be polite. "Thank you for supper."

"Of course. I'm sure we'll be seeing each other in passing again soon. But, perhaps next time, when Knox and the girls come by, you might choose to stay home?"

Without another word, Merritt left Penelope's patio and walked through the darkening yard to Knox's house, heat filling her cheeks while her pulse thrummed in her veins. Penelope's words and behavior left her feeling shaky and unsettled. She had fought against these thoughts and beliefs all her life, hoping that they weren't true but always wondering if there was some truth to them. She *felt* simple and plain. Maybe the reason she'd never gone after a man like Knox was because she knew they would never be interested in her. It was easier to reject him before he had a chance to reject her.

Then why did Penelope's words hurt so much? Why did she care what Penelope said? Didn't she tell her kindergarten students that they should be proud of who they were and not let other people determine their self-worth? So then why did she let Penelope's words seep so easily into the crevices of her heart?

Knox's house was dark as she let herself into the kitchen. Darby got up and stretched, so Merritt let her out the back door, all the while watching for Knox and the girls to come home.

After Darby did what she needed to do, she came back inside and went to her water dish.

And, still, Knox and the girls didn't come home.

The sun set, and Merritt turned on the kitchen lights, her heart heavy, wondering why Knox wasn't back yet. Had he decided to stay, now that Merritt was no longer there? Maybe he had wanted to be alone with Penelope the whole time and had only been polite to include her?

It was past the girls' bedtime, and Merritt was beginning to feel foolish for sitting in the kitchen and waiting for them. Who knew how long it might be before they came home?

She went up to her room, checked her phone to see if she had missed any calls or emails and then put on a pair of yoga pants and a sweatshirt before pulling her laptop out of its bag to work on her résumé.

It was another half an hour before she heard commotion in the hallway.

"It's way past your bedtime, girls," Knox said quietly as they walked past her door. "You can play with Veronica tomorrow."

Did he need help getting them to bed? If so, he didn't bother to knock on her door and ask.

For some reason, Merritt felt upset that Knox had stayed so much longer at Penelope's—and that he was promising the girls they could play with Veronica tomorrow. That meant seeing Penelope again. Merritt hated to admit the feeling was jealousy, because she had no reason to be jealous. Knox didn't belong to her—she hardly knew him, and he didn't owe her anything. She told herself it was because she didn't like or trust Penelope, but Knox was a big boy. He shouldn't need Merritt telling him whom he could see or not see—even if it did impact her nieces.

"I want Auntie Merritt to pray for us," one of the girls said, her voice muffled by the door.

"Don't bother your aunt," Knox told her. "She's probably in bed."

Merritt set aside her laptop and stood, not wanting to miss the opportunity to say good-night and pray for the girls, especially if they wanted her to.

"I'm not in bed," Merritt said as she opened the door and found the trio about to enter the girls' room down the hall.

Blair and Addison smiled, but Merritt didn't bother to look for Knox's reaction. She didn't even glance up at him as she helped the girls into their pajamas and then into bed.

After she prayed for them and kissed them both good-night, she left their bedroom.

She didn't bother to acknowledge Knox the whole time. He didn't owe her an explanation, but she wanted one. Wanted to know why he had chosen to stay after she left.

But she would never ask.

She walked down the hall, toward her bedroom, and was about to turn the doorknob when Knox exited the girls' room.

"Why did you leave without us?" he asked gently,

walking toward her. "I was hoping to come back here and enjoy the sunset with you."

His words surprised her. "Then why did you wait so long to come home?"

"I couldn't get away from Penelope. She kept finding one excuse after another to prevent me from coming home."

"Why didn't you just leave?" Merritt's voice betrayed her dislike of Penelope. She couldn't help it. The woman had been insulting.

"I didn't want to be rude." He stepped a little closer to her and leaned up against the wall next to her door.

The hallway was shadowed and felt far too intimate. He smelled amazing and looked even better. Merritt's pulse raced, and she forced herself to look away from him.

"Are you mad at me?" he asked.

She had no right to be mad at him—and she wasn't. Her pain had come from Penelope, and the resulting anger had transferred to Knox when he had chosen to spend time with Penelope. But it was pointless to hold him accountable for her harsh words.

"No," she finally said.

"Why did you leave?"

It felt catty to make Penelope look bad in Knox's eyes, so there was no point in sharing what the other woman had said. "I didn't think you needed my help getting home."

"Maybe I didn't need your help, but I would have enjoyed your company."

His words were so soft, so inviting, Merritt's heart quickened as she met his gaze.

He smiled, watching her in the dim light. "I was disappointed when I found out you left. And now I'm even more disappointed that we missed the sunset together. I was looking forward to enjoying it with you all day."

Had he? Joy bubbled up in her heart. "There's always tomorrow."

"I'll hold you to it," he said. "Tomorrow, sunset, my patio?"

She nodded, looking forward to all the sunsets they'd get to watch together this summer—already feeling like there wouldn't be enough.

Chapter Seven

It was amazing how quickly the first week flew by for Merritt, especially with the work on the playhouse taking up so much of their time. When Saturday arrived, she stepped out of her bedroom ready to roll her sleeves up and help wherever she was needed.

But Knox had a different plan.

"Good morning," he said to her when she entered the kitchen.

The girls had not come down for breakfast yet, but Knox looked ready for them. He'd made pancakes, filled their cups with orange juice and was cutting up strawberries. The smell of fresh-brewed coffee lingered in the air, and he'd already pulled out a couple of mugs, which were sitting next to the coffee maker.

"Good morning," she said, stifling a yawn with her hand. "You're up early. Who do you have lined up to come out to the construction site today?"

"No one." He set a pile of sliced strawberries on each of the girls' plates. "We're not working on the playhouse today."

"We're not?" Merritt went to the coffee maker and

poured them each a cup. She added a splash of hazelnut creamer to hers and a splash of regular creamer to his. "What are you doing today?"

"*We*—" he emphasized the word as he took the mug she offered "—are going on a field trip today—if you'd like to."

"A field trip?" Merritt smiled, thinking about all the field trips she'd taken with her students over the years. The word always held a dose of excitement and anxiety. She loved taking the students to unique places to teach them about fun and interesting things—but it usually involved a lot of stress and planning on her part. "Are we going to the zoo? A museum? A park?"

"Not quite." His eyes sparkled with mischief.

"Not quite a zoo, a museum or a park?"

"No."

"Those are three very different things."

"Not really. Not in this case."

His words intrigued her, and the look of pleasure in his smile warmed her all the way through. It was amazing how much she had come to love that smile of his and the way it lit up his eyes.

The girls were soon downstairs and everyone was fed, then they quickly got dressed, let Darby out one more time and then piled into Knox's SUV. The girls were buckled into their booster seats, and then Knox pulled out of the garage.

"Do we need to take along anything special?" Merritt asked him for the third or fourth time that morning? "Snacks? Water toys? Sunscreen?"

"Not today." He smiled, offering another evasive answer. "I've got everything under control."

Merritt threw up her hands in defeat, laughter in her

voice. "If you say so." It was nice not to have to worry about the details.

The girls chatted all the way into Timber Falls. It was about a twenty-minute drive, past farm fields, pastureland and well-manicured lawns. Merritt loved being back in Minnesota. Every so often, they passed a body of water, whether a lake, pond, stream or river, and she marveled at the diversity in the landscape. Tall, majestic trees, hills and lowlands all filled the space between Tucker Lake and Timber Falls.

"Won't you give me any hints?" Merritt asked.

"None."

She gave up trying and instead spent time listening to Knox talk about his childhood. It seemed almost idyllic and paired with many of the experiences Merritt had had as a child. Camping trips, vacations, family reunions—they really had more in common than Merritt would have initially suspected. Knox loved his parents and sister and was close to his extended family. Merritt was close to hers, as well—with the exception of Reina, who chose not to be a part of their family. Reina had never been close to their father, though he had tried to bridge whatever gap she had placed between them.

Both Knox and Merritt had grown up with strong faith and a close connection to their churches. They'd both been encouraged to get a higher education and had chosen colleges close to their homes.

The more she got to know him, the more she liked him—and the more she wondered what had attracted him to Reina. From everything he told her, he longed for the kind of life Merritt wanted for herself—one that would have been repulsive to Reina.

"We're almost there," Knox said as they drove through downtown Timber Falls.

Merritt watched the passing storefronts and marveled at the Mississippi River as it wound its way through the small town. A charming park hugged the shoreline of the river and boasted a pavilion, meandering paths and green lampposts. It looked like an event was being set up near the pavilion.

"It looks like a wedding—or a festival of some kind," Merritt mentioned as she pointed at the park, which sloped down from the main road.

Knox glanced in the direction she pointed but didn't comment. Instead, he put on his blinker and turned into a large estate nearby.

A fence encircled the immense property, and trees lined the private drive. A pool house and tennis court appeared on her right as a historic mansion materialized through the trees ahead. The white clapboard siding was broken up by the large windows and charming angles, hinting at a turn-of-the-century construction date.

"Where are we?" Merritt asked.

"We're at Noah Asher's home," he said with a smile. "His town house."

"Noah Asher?" Merritt turned to look at Knox. "As in, the lumber baron who built the little cabin on your property?"

"The very same."

"I thought you said he died."

"He did, but the house is still in the family. His great-grandson Chase Asher now manages the estate. Chase and his wife, Joy, operate a special nonprofit organization in our community for widows and orphans.

I've been a donor since they started, and they've been encouraging me to come and meet them. The girls know their children from church. When I emailed them and said you were interested in learning more about Noah Asher, they told me to bring you by today. Joy created a whole room in the mansion dedicated to their family history. It's just like a museum and the property is like a park."

Merritt's mouth slipped open at the news. "That was so thoughtful, Knox. But I don't want anyone to go to any trouble for me."

"It's no trouble, Merritt." His smile was sweet as he looked her way. "I've been wanting to meet the Ashers, and the girls will enjoy playing with their friends."

Even though he made excuses for why they'd come, she had a strong suspicion that the real reason was because she had shown so much interest in learning more about Noah Asher and the history of Tucker Lake. It warmed her heart that he had made it happen.

Knox pulled to a stop in front of the massive house, and the front door opened almost immediately. A whole passel of children came down the stairs and out onto the driveway. Merritt quickly counted three older boys and two identical little girls.

"And here's the zoo," Knox laughed.

"Harper!" Blair called through the closed car door as she struggled to get out of her seat belt. "Kinsley!"

"Chase and Joy Asher have identical twin girls a little bit older than mine," Knox said to Merritt. "Mrs. Masterson has told me many stories about the two sets of twins over the past couple of years. They're the best of friends, and they'll all enter Timber Falls Community Christian School in the fall together."

Blair and Addison were soon out of the SUV and greeting their friends. The Asher twins had dark brown hair and eyes, creating a distinct contrast between Blair and Addison's blond hair and blue eyes. But they were all about the same height. It was fun seeing two sets of identical twins together.

"The boys are adopted," Knox said as Merritt unlocked her seat belt. "And, from what Mrs. Masterson has told me, the Ashers also have a baby boy together."

"Wow." Merritt's eyebrows rose in surprise. "I'm impressed. I thought one set of twin girls was a handful. Could you imagine having three older boys and a baby?"

They both exited the car and greeted the other children, then the girls asked if they could play with Harper and Kinsley on their swing set. Knox gave them permission and then motioned for Merritt to precede him up the steps to the front door. It led onto a wide, covered porch, where another door awaited. This one was thicker and made of a beautiful quarter-sawn oak.

Knox rang the doorbell, and it was soon answered by a beautiful young woman with a wide smile.

"Knox?" she asked, her brown eyes shining with welcome. "And you must be Merritt?"

Merritt nodded.

"I'm Joy Asher," she said. "Welcome to Bee Tree Hill. Won't you come in?" She opened the door and motioned for them to enter an elegant foyer.

"I heard the kids leave the house," Joy said. "I'm assuming they've already whisked Blair and Addison off to their play set?"

Knox nodded and grinned. "We had quite the welcome."

Joy laughed, and Merritt immediately liked her. She was kind and warm, and though she was beautiful, she seemed very down-to-earth and oblivious to her charm. If Merritt had to guess, she would assume that Joy was about the same age as she was, though her six children might indicate otherwise.

A handsome man came down the stairs with a folder in hand and a smile on his face. He joined Joy as he extended a hand to Knox and then to Merritt. "I'm Chase," he said. "It's nice to finally meet you."

For some reason, Merritt felt a little starstruck in Chase's presence, knowing he was Noah Asher's great-grandson. It didn't make any sense to her, but it was still amazing to know that this man's ancestor had played such an important part of the history of the area.

"Thank you for having us," Knox said, watching Merritt's expression, a smile still playing about his face. "We're both excited to learn more about Noah Asher and the foundation you've created in your family's name."

"I thought we could start by taking a little tour of the house," Joy said, "if you'd like."

"I'd love that." Merritt finally found her voice. "It doesn't look like it's changed since it was built."

"We've worked hard to keep its historical integrity," Chase said. "But we have six children, so it's been a little harder than you might think."

"I'm a kindergarten teacher," Merritt told him. "I completely understand."

Joy's face lit up. "I'm an elementary school social worker—or, that is, I used to be. I resigned right before our youngest, Shepherd, was born. I hope to return one day when the kids are a bit older."

"Maybe you know of a job in the area," Knox said to Joy. "Merritt is currently looking for a new position, and I could use someone's help trying to convince her to stay in Timber Falls."

Merritt turned to Knox, unable to hide the surprise from her face. He wanted her to stay in Timber Falls?

He met her gaze but didn't hide the hope that lighted his eyes.

"Actually," Joy said, "I did hear a rumor about one of the teachers at the Christian school. I'll check into it and see if the position opened."

Merritt was about to tell her there was no need, because she hadn't even considered staying in Timber Falls, when Chase handed Merritt a folder.

"This is my own personal file I've collected about my great-grandfather Noah." He opened the front flap and pointed at a picture. "This was Noah and his wife, Julia Morgan, on their wedding day in 1898. She was a music teacher from New York City. They had an incredible love story, which you'll find in the letters in the file. Take it with you and look it over. I think you'll enjoy it."

"I couldn't possibly take this from you," Merritt said, trying to hand it back.

Chase lifted his hands and shook his head. "I insist. What's the point in having information if you're not willing to share it? Maybe, after you read through the file, you'll start to appreciate Timber Falls all the more because of what it took to establish this town."

"And maybe we'll convince you to apply for that teaching position," Joy said with a wink.

Merritt closed the folder and held it against her chest as she met Knox's gaze once again.

How was it possible that she was falling for both him *and* this charming community at the same time?

But, more importantly, how could she stop it from happening?

Knox loved meeting the Ashers and loved, even more, watching Merritt soak up all the information they shared with her about Noah Asher and the legacy he had left in Timber Falls. The home and grounds were amazing, and their hospitality was beyond anything Knox had expected.

But Knox's favorite part of the day was yet to come, and he had Joy Asher to thank for it.

"Well," Knox said as he put his hands on his knees and pushed his chair away from the dining room table where they'd been looking over old pictures in the Asher family collection. "We should probably get going."

"Do the girls know about the surprise yet?" Joy asked.

"I mentioned it to them before we left the house," Knox said. "Their overnight bags are in the back of the SUV."

"Overnight bags?" Merritt asked.

"The girls are having their first sleepover," Knox told her. "Joy asked if they'd like to stay with Harper and Kinsley, and she offered to take them to church in the morning. We'll pick them up there."

Merritt blinked several times but didn't say anything. Her dimples deepened as she pressed her lips together.

After Knox and Merritt said goodbye to the girls

and to the Ashers, they got into his SUV and pulled out of Bee Tree Hill.

"You're a little quiet," Knox said, turning left onto Main Street.

"It's just—" She paused and clasped her hands together in her lap. "Won't it be strange to be at the house…without them?"

"I'll miss them, but I thought it would be fun to take the evening off. There's an old movie festival at the park tonight. I thought maybe we could stop there and eat at one of the food trucks and then watch the movie. They're showing *Two to Tango*, starring Esther Lund and John Hawthorn."

Merritt looked out the window, her hands still clasped tight in her lap. He thought she would have embraced an evening without the girls—especially watching an old movie. They had spent hours talking about their favorites, and many of them had featured Esther Lund, a famous movie star who had grown up in Timber Falls in the early part of the twentieth century. But Merritt clearly didn't look as pleased as he had hoped. Maybe it felt too much like a date to her. Why hadn't he considered that when he'd made the plans? Of course she wouldn't want to go on a date with him. They had a lot of summer left, and it could make things really complicated and uncomfortable if she thought he was trying to date her.

"We don't have to go to the festival," he said quickly. "If you'd rather we just head back out to the lake for the evening, we can do that."

She swallowed. "It'll be awfully quiet at the house—without the girls there."

He suddenly realized why she was feeling uncomfortable. They'd just left the girls at the Ashers', which meant they'd be all alone at the house tonight—alone together.

Knox turned left to go down the hill toward the festival parking lot. Hundreds of people milled about the park, smoke and steam rose from the dozen food trucks, and the river sparkled beyond it all.

"I guess I didn't think through the logistics of the whole thing," he said with an awkward laugh. "If you're uncomfortable being in the house alone with me, I can always sleep on the hammock, under the stars. I've been wanting to go camping for a while."

"I'm not going to make you sleep outside tonight," she said, finally looking at him. "We're adults. It doesn't have to be weird."

Knox parked the car and turned off the engine. He was suddenly nervous, being alone with her. They didn't have the distraction of the girls or the playhouse project. It was just the two of them. What if they couldn't find anything to talk about?

Or what if they enjoyed it too much? In the week he'd spent with Merritt, he'd come to like her more and more. Each new day he'd discovered a different facet of her personality, and each one was more endearing than the one before.

He studied her and she looked back at him, her brown eyes both leery and hopeful at the same time.

"Do you want to stop at the festival?" he asked. "Or would you rather go home? It's your night off. You can make the call."

"I think the festival sounds like fun." She laid her hand on his forearm, her voice sincere. "Thank you for planning it for me, Knox. It was really thoughtful."

Heat traveled up his arm and filled his chest at the pressure of her hand on his arm. He wanted to cover her hand with his own as a rush of affection filled him. She was becoming very dear to him, more so than he'd ever expected. In one short week, she felt like family. Like she belonged with them. She'd slipped effortlessly into his home—and heart.

The realization surprised him and he inhaled, but she lifted her hand from his arm and said, "I'm starving. What truck should we visit first?" She didn't seem fazed by the touch as she opened the door to get out of the SUV.

He sat for a second to catch his breath and still his thoughts. He couldn't allow the feelings he had for her to grow. If he wasn't careful, he could fall in love with Merritt Lane. It would be easy—easier than anything had ever been in his life. Being with her was effortless. He looked forward to each new day. From the moment they greeted each other to the moment they said goodnight, he craved not only her companionship but also her thoughts and opinions.

Already, he missed her when he thought about her returning to South Carolina. How would he go back to life as normal after knowing her and realizing what an incredible person she was?

Knox got out of his car and joined her, admiring the way her dimples shined as she inspected the festival.

"Every time I turn around," she said, "I'm finding more and more reasons to love Timber Falls. This community is amazing. I love that Esther Lund grew up here."

"I've been to a lot of places in my life," Knox said,

feeling a little pride for his hometown, "and none of them quite compare to Timber Falls."

"I can see why."

They walked to the food truck lane and looked over all the menus before settling on Indian tacos from one truck and Greek gyros from another. Knox bought fresh-squeezed lemonade, and they took their food to a picnic table near the river, where they settled in to enjoy their supper.

"You're even more of a foodie than I am," Knox said to Merritt, impressed with her knowledge of the different culinary options they had to choose from.

"It's one of my dreams to take a trip around the world, just to sample all the different cuisines."

"That sounds like my kind of vacation." Knox grinned and set down the large glasses of lemonade. He smiled at an older couple he recognized and then turned his full attention back to Merritt. They said a simple blessing over the food and then split the taco and the gyro to each have half.

"One of the things I was most looking forward to on my honeymoon was the food." Merritt lifted her plastic fork, a sheepish smile on her face. "Does that sound bad?"

"Yes." Knox returned her smile, feeling it all the way to the tips of his toes.

Merritt dipped her head in embarrassment.

Knox laughed, and she playfully nudged his foot with her own underneath the table.

When his laughter died down, and after they'd taken a few bites of food, Knox ventured into uncharted territory. "May I ask what went wrong between you and Brad?"

A gentle breeze blew off the river, ruffling Merritt's dark brown hair and tossing it around her shoulders. She often wore it up in a ponytail while at the lake but had worn it down today. It looked so thick and glossy.

She moved her food around with her fork for a second before meeting his gaze. "The truth?"

"Of course." He didn't take another bite, waiting to hear what she would say.

"He wasn't the one."

Her statement hit him square in the chest, and he couldn't help but wonder who Merritt's "one" could be. A strange sense of jealousy hovered over him as he thought about her with another man. He forced himself to ask, "Then why did you hold on to him for so long?"

"Because I'm just realizing the truth now."

"You would have gone through with the wedding?"

She nodded. "I would have. And I would have made it work with him, too. When I get married, it will be for life."

Even though he had been part of a failed marriage, he didn't feel like her comment was a slight against him. He knew she was sincere. She was the kind of person that would stick with the people she committed to through thick or thin.

"I hate what he did to you," Knox said quietly.

She was silent for another moment, and then she let out a sigh. "He probably realized what I'm just now seeing. We weren't right together." Her eyes were filled with so much pain, he wished he could pull her into his arms and fight off the hurt for her. But all he could do was watch and listen.

"It's taken me a long time to realize that I've always looked for the wrong kind of man—at least for me. I had a certain type in mind—one just like Brad. Reliable. Predictable."

"Boring?" Knox asked, trying to lighten the mood.

"Safe," she offered and then sighed. "I wasn't really looking for someone spontaneous or exciting."

Knox frowned. "Why not?"

She pressed her lips together as she studied him for a heartbeat. "I didn't want to go after the type of men Reina was drawn to, because I didn't want to be anything like her. I still don't."

He didn't say anything for a moment as the truth sank in. She didn't want someone Reina would choose—someone like him.

"But you realize now that you were wrong to choose Brad?" Knox asked.

"I was wrong to choose him just because he wasn't someone my sister would date." She laid her fork down. "But that doesn't mean that I was completely wrong. Reina dated a lot of bad guys over the years. I told myself a long time ago that I wouldn't do the same thing."

Had Merritt clumped Knox into that group? Did she think he was bad?

"But Brad hurt you in the end," he reminded her gently, trying hard not to take her words personally. He knew her well enough to know that she wasn't trying to insult him.

She studied Knox and shook her head. "He simply had the courage to walk away when he realized we were all wrong together."

Which was exactly what Reina had done.

The realization washed over Knox like a tidal wave. Yes, Reina had hurt him—and she'd chosen to end things in a way that would have catastrophic conse-

quences in his daughters' lives for years to come—
but she had known they weren't right for each other.
The only difference was that Knox would have tried to
make it work. He was just like Merritt. Once he made
a commitment, he was in it for life.

It didn't make things easier, but for the first time, he
had a better understanding of Reina and her choices.

Chapter Eight

The house was dark as Merritt followed Knox inside from the garage. He flipped on the entryway light and held the door open for her.

Darby was there to greet them, her feet prancing on the stone floor and her tail wagging in delight.

Merritt smiled at Knox as she passed him, her heart warm from the evening they spent next to the river, under the stars, watching Esther Lund's character falling in love with the handsome John Hawthorn.

There had hardly been a lull in the conversation all day. Merritt was amazed at how much they had to talk about—as if they were trying to make up for the years they hadn't known one another.

But there was one thing they hadn't discussed—their relationship. Maybe it was because there was nothing to say. They were becoming friends—good friends—and that was all it could be.

Merritt hung her oversize purse on the coat tree and then reached down to pet Darby. The house seemed so quiet without the girls—too quiet.

Even though Merritt and Knox had been alone all

the way home in the car, there was something much different about being alone in the house. They had been able to talk all the way. But now, as they arrived at the empty house, their aloneness felt a lot different to Merritt.

"Are you tired?" he asked as he closed the door and tossed the keys onto the hall table.

"Not really." Their conversation had been stimulating, and after a day of so much of it, she didn't think she'd fall asleep for hours.

"Can I show you something?" he asked.

"Sure." The last time he'd asked her that, he'd shown her where he was putting the playhouse, and she'd been pleasantly surprised.

They let Darby outside and filled her water and food dishes and then let her back in before Knox opened the back door again and tilted his head toward the lake. "It's out here."

Merritt wrapped her cardigan a little closer around her body as she followed him outside and into the cool air once again.

The stars were magnificent out over the lake, without a cloud in the sky. The moon was nowhere to be seen, allowing the stars to shine even brighter.

She didn't ask where they were going as she walked beside him toward the dock. It was wide enough for the two of them to walk next to each other, the heels of their shoes tapping on the cedarwood planks until they reached the end.

Knox sat down, and Merritt followed. They sat close—their legs pressed together as their feet hung over the edge, just above the water. But neither one made a move to pull away.

It was so quiet and peaceful. There wasn't a single boat on the dark lake, yet there were several lights on in the houses rimming it.

"What are we looking at?" Merritt asked on a whisper, her voice matching the sound of the gentle waves as they lapped against the dock.

Knox leaned around her and pointed to a place on the horizon to her right.

Merritt turned to look over her shoulder, and her breath caught.

A brilliant display of green lights shot up into the sky, waving and shimmering in all their grandeur.

"It's the aurora borealis, or northern lights," Knox said. "I heard they might be shining tonight and I caught a glimpse of them on the way here, but I wanted you to see them for the first time like this."

He was close as he pressed up against her to get a good look.

"I've never seen them before," she breathed, more aware of him than the northern lights. He smelled wonderful this close.

A streak of purple shot up through the green, and the waves of light shifted, almost looking like colorful mountains. It was incredible.

"This world will never cease to amaze me," Knox said. "I've only seen the northern lights a handful of times in my life, but each time, they look a little different. Some people travel hundreds or thousands of miles to see these—and we get to watch them from the end of our dock."

Our dock.

Merritt liked the way Knox had included her in the

ownership of the dock, though this was not her home. It made her feel welcomed—included—wanted.

"Here," Knox said as he turned and faced her on the dock. "We might be more comfortable if we're facing them."

Merritt moved from the end of the dock to sit beside him, crossing her legs to be more comfortable.

Knox leaned back on his elbows in a semi-reclined position. "I think I might actually sleep on the hammock tonight," he said. "The weather is perfect, and I can fall asleep watching the northern lights."

Smiling, Merritt nudged him with her shoulder. "You don't have to sleep outside."

"I'm serious. I haven't slept under the stars since I was a kid. It could be fun."

A firework shot up into the sky from down the shoreline and exploded in a profusion of green and pink lights.

Merritt jumped at the suddenness of the display, but the joy in seeing it made her adrenaline quiet.

One after the other, a beautiful show was put on for them, and neither one said anything for a moment.

"What do you think is the occasion?" Merritt asked.

"The Fourth of July is next week. A lot of people like to start celebrating early. Next weekend there will be a dozen displays just like it. We can take out the pontoon with the girls and watch them from the lake."

Merritt's smile widened. She couldn't wait to see the girls' reaction—and she loved the idea of spending that time with Knox.

More and more, she was looking forward to these moments with him. Whether with the girls or not, she loved how she felt when they were together. Just thinking about leaving him and the girls in six weeks was too much to bear, so she tried not to think about it.

This was just a summer vacation. A break from reality. But, at the end, she would be back in South Carolina, teaching, and trying to pick up the pieces of her life there. Unless—unless she didn't go back.

"Were you serious today when you asked Joy about a teaching job for me in Timber Falls?"

Knox nodded. "Very serious."

"Would you truly like me to stay?"

"I think all of us would like you to stay. The girls don't have any relatives around here, and they've grown to love you. I hate to think about how much they'll miss you."

It wasn't the reason she'd hoped—but what could he have said? That *he* wanted her to stay? That *he'd* miss her?

"Do you want to stay?" he asked

"I haven't given it much thought. My life is in South Carolina. All that's here for me are the girls—and even though I love them dearly, I don't know if I can give up everything for them."

He looked down at his feet and nodded, as if he was disappointed by her answer.

Neither one spoke for another minute until Knox said quietly, "Merritt?"

She met his gaze—and her breath caught. There was something vulnerable in the way he looked at her.

"Do you still think I'm one of the bad guys?"

His question was so unexpected—so personal—it took her by surprise. What had made him wonder? Was it their conversation at the park when she'd told him why she didn't date men like the kind Reina dated?

It didn't matter why he was asking. She knew her answer. She'd been all wrong about him, so she shook her head. "No."

His smile was warm and a bit disarming, but he didn't say anything as he returned his gaze to the northern lights.

"What about me?" she asked, almost afraid to know what he really thought about her. "Do you still think I'm like my sister?"

When he met her gaze again, his face was filled with a look of affection that made her heart pound.

"I've never met anyone like you, Merritt Lane, and I don't think I ever will again. You're nothing like what I expected and so much more than I could have ever hoped."

She couldn't stop the smile that formed on her face, nor wipe it off when she knew she was grinning like a buffoon. She couldn't help it, so she had to look away from him, her cheeks growing warm. No one had ever told her something that sweet before.

But it also embarrassed her, and she knew that if she allowed it to get too serious, they'd both get uncomfortable, so she nudged him again playfully and kept her voice neutral when she said, "That's the nicest thing anyone has ever said to me."

"Well, it's true." Thankfully, he kept it light, too. "I'm happy you came. We might have gone our whole lives believing things about each other that weren't true."

Merritt was happy she'd come, too. And she was thankful they were getting to know one another, but it came with a price. The more she knew Knox, the more she liked him. The more she liked him, the more she fell for him. And she was falling fast.

But it didn't change one thing—the most important thing.

Reina had fallen first.

Knox rubbed his neck as he and Merritt entered Timber Falls Community Church. He had been serious the night before when he told Merritt he was going to sleep in the hammock—and he did. But today he was regretting that decision. It hadn't been as comfortable as he would have liked, and the mosquitoes had come out in the middle of the night, buzzing around his head, waking him up every time he was finally asleep. The awkward position he'd lain in had left a crick in his neck that was still aching.

But all of it had been worth it, knowing Merritt had felt a little more peace of mind in the house by herself.

And after the conversation they'd had on the dock, he knew he needed to give them both a little space.

He was falling for Merritt, and despite his best efforts, he couldn't stop his feelings from growing. The trouble was, he didn't want to stop himself from falling, though he knew it was a bad idea. His instincts told him to run—and run fast. There was nothing but heartache on the end of any relationship he had ever attempted—the worst being with Merritt's sister. Because of the family connection, things were so much more complicated.

But he couldn't leave like he used to. He had promised the girls he'd be there to help them build the playhouse. He could send Merritt away, but that was a jerk move, too. He still needed her help, and he'd promised her a place to crash for the summer.

His best course of action was to ignore the feelings, stop putting himself in intimate situations with her and hope and pray he could survive until she left in August.

So far, he was failing miserably.

"Daddy!" Blair and Addison both called out to him when they saw him enter the church building.

They were smiling as they ran up to him. Blair jumped into his arms while Addison grabbed him around his leg and hugged tight.

"Did you have a good sleepover?" he asked them.

They both began to talk at the same time, and Knox laughed, sharing a smile with Merritt, who listened intently to their stories. Any trace of uneasiness he felt about letting them have their first sleepover vanished.

Joy and Chase Asher walked up behind them. Joy was holding Shepherd, who was almost a year and a half. They'd met the little guy at the Ashers' home the day before, but he'd been cranky after his nap. Today, he was grinning and trying to wiggle out of his mother's arms to join the bigger kids as they played with their friends in the fellowship hall outside the sanctuary.

"Thank you for letting them sleep over," Knox said to Joy and Chase. "I'm sure they'll be full of stories all day."

"It was our pleasure," Joy said. "They're welcome anytime."

Merritt stood next to Knox, a little quieter than usual as she looked around the room. She had been reserved that morning and hadn't said much on their way into town from the lake. He wished he knew what was both-

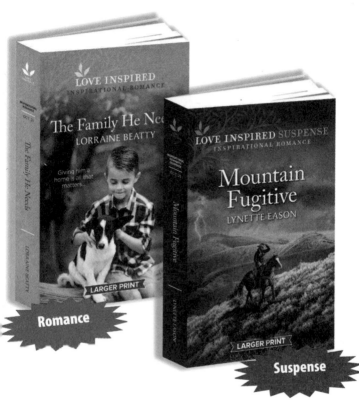

Get ready to relax and indulge with your FREE BOOKS and more!

Claim up to FOUR NEW BOOKS & TWO MYSTERY GIFTS – absolutely FREE!

Dear Reader,

We both know life can be difficult at times. That's why it's important to treat yourself so you can relax and recharge once in a while.

And I'd like to help you do this by sending you this amazing offer of up to FOUR brand new full length FREE BOOKS that WE pay for.

This is everything I have ready to send to you right now:

Try **Love Inspired® Romance Larger-Print** books and fall in love with inspirational romances that take you on an uplifting journey of faith, forgiveness and hope.

Try **Love Inspired® Suspense Larger-Print** books where courage and optimism unite in stories of faith and love in the face of danger.

Or **TRY BOTH!**

All we ask in return is that you answer 4 simple questions on the attached Treat Yourself survey. You'll get **Two Free Books** and **Two Mystery Gifts** from each series you try, *altogether worth over $20!* Who could pass up a deal like that?

Sincerely,

Pam Powers

Harlequin Reader Service

Treat Yourself to Free Books and Free Gifts.

Answer 4 fun questions and get rewarded.

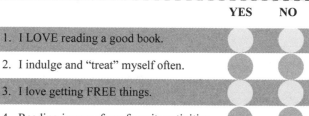

**We love to connect with our readers!
Please tell us a little about you...**

◄ DETACH AND MAIL CARD TODAY! ►

	YES	NO
1. I LOVE reading a good book.		
2. I indulge and "treat" myself often.		
3. I love getting FREE things.		
4. Reading is one of my favorite activities.		

TREAT YOURSELF • Pick your 2 Free Books...

Yes! Please send me my Free Books from each series I select and Free Mystery Gifts. I understand that I am under no obligation to buy anything, as explained on the back of this card.

Which do you prefer?

❏ **Love Inspired® Romance Larger-Print** 122/322 IDL GRDP
❏ **Love Inspired® Suspense Larger-Print** 107/307 IDL GRDP
❏ **Try Both** 122/322 & 107/307 IDL GRED

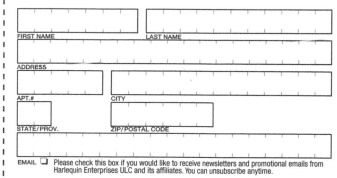

FIRST NAME   LAST NAME

ADDRESS

APT.#   CITY

STATE/PROV.   ZIP/POSTAL CODE

EMAIL ❏ Please check this box if you would like to receive newsletters and promotional emails from Harlequin Enterprises ULC and its affiliates. You can unsubscribe anytime.

© 2022 HARLEQUIN ENTERPRISES ULC
"" and ® are trademarks owned by Harlequin Enterprises ULC. Printed in the U.S.A.

LI/SLI-520-TY22

ering her, but he hadn't been too talkative himself after the night on the hammock.

"Merritt," Joy said as she handed Shepherd off to her husband, "have you met Max and Piper Evans?"

"I don't believe I have."

Joy motioned to a couple who had just entered, one whom Knox had known most of his life.

He grinned, still impressed with his old classmate Max, who had played professional football for several years before coming back to Timber Falls to coach the high school team and marry his longtime sweetheart, Piper.

"Knox!" Piper said when she caught his eye. She was holding a baby girl on her hip, and though Knox had a hard time estimating the ages of babies, he would guess that this one wasn't old enough to walk yet.

"Hi, Piper." Knox gave her a side hug and then reached out and shook Max's hand. "It's good to see you both again."

They'd graduated the year after him, but they'd all been part of the same friend group.

"Max and Piper," Joy said, "I'd like to introduce you to Merritt Lane. She's here helping Knox with the girls this summer."

"It's so nice to meet you," Piper said with a smile for Merritt. "I hope you're enjoying your time in Timber Falls."

"It's been wonderful, especially at the lake. I could get used to this lifestyle."

Piper glanced at Knox, probably wondering about the connection between him and Merritt. He just smiled, not willing to tell her about Reina—at least not now, with Merritt standing there. Anytime he brought up her sister's name, he could see it upset her. The more he'd come to know Merritt, the more he realized there was bad blood between the sisters. But he hadn't gotten up the nerve to ask too many questions. They'd both avoided talking about Reina as much as possible.

"Here's Liv and Zane," Piper said as she waved at another familiar person.

Knox smiled when he saw Liv Butler. She'd been in the same grade as Max and Piper and had moved to Timber Falls the summer after Knox had graduated. He'd had a crush on her those few short months and had often wondered about her. Everything about Liv proclaimed style and grace. At her side was a man Knox hadn't met, and they were followed by two girls. One of them looked like she was eleven or twelve, but the other was closer in age to Blair and Addison.

"Knox Taylor!" Liv said as her eyes opened wide. "It's been years." She came up to him and gave him a big hug. "Where have you been keeping yourself these days? We see the girls all the time with Mrs. Masterson, but have had to wonder about you."

"I'm at the lake this summer," he said, feeling the weight of the past five years bearing down on him. All these people knew his daughters, but they hardly saw him. They were good friends who had been left in the dust—yet they were welcoming him back with open arms.

"Liv Butler," Knox said, "this is my—" He was at a loss, again, as to how to introduce Merritt. "My ex-sister-in-law." It was the truth, though it felt far too impersonal. Merritt was so much more to him. "Merritt Lane. She's here to help with the girls for the summer."

Merritt extended her hand to shake Liv's, her smile

looking a bit uncomfortable. Was she upset at being referred to as his ex-sister-in-law, or was she feeling overwhelmed meeting all these people? "It's nice to meet you."

"It's actually Liv Harris now," she said with a smile. "And this is my husband, Zane." Liv wrapped her arm through her husband's. "And our daughters, Miley and Alexis."

Knox shook Zane's hand, surprised at how much the older girl looked like Liv. But surely the girls must be her stepdaughters, since the last time Knox had seen Liv, just a few years ago, she hadn't been married— or had children.

"It's a long story," Liv said to Knox when she saw his curious look. "We'll invite you over sometime and tell you all about it."

Zane winked at his wife from behind his glasses as the doors to the sanctuary were being opened by the pastor.

"We'll introduce you to the pastor and his wife after the service," Joy said to Knox and Merritt. "You'll love Jacob and Kate. Kate used to be a Broadway actress before she came to Timber Falls. They have a set of identical triplets." She grinned. "We're all part of a mothers-of-multiples group here in town. You should come sometime, Merritt."

"I'm not a mother of multiples," Merritt said quickly. "I'm not a mother at all."

"You don't have to be a mom," Joy amended. "Mrs. Masterson joins us once in a while. We really should change the name of the group. It's more like a group for caregivers of multiples. We meet here at the church once a month and cover lots of topics specific to parenting twins and triplets."

Merritt glanced at Knox, and he thought he saw a hint of longing in her face. Did she want to be a mom? The only clue she'd given was that first night, sitting on the patio, when she'd said that Reina was wrong to give up the house, the kids and him. But had she been speaking in generalities? If her plans had succeeded, she would have been settling into married life this summer—probably hoping to start a family soon. It must be hard for her to be around all these people her age who were in the midst of growing their families. Especially when she was so amazing with kids. Her patience and creativity with them were boundless. He'd witnessed it firsthand, over and over again.

He smiled at her and then caught Joy's eye before they walked into the sanctuary.

"I'm wondering if you could do me a favor," he said to Joy before he forgot. "Merritt and I are hoping to have a birthday party for the girls in August. Could you email me a list of names and addresses for Blair and Addison's friends? I feel like I'm playing catch-up here and I don't want to miss anyone that would like to come and celebrate with them."

"I'd be happy to send you a list. I actually have one from the last birthday party we had for our girls. Most of their friends are the same."

"Thank you. I'd really appreciate it."

"I'm actually going to be out by your place tomorrow," Liv said to Knox. "I have a potential client I'm going to meet. She just moved to the area and would like an interior designer's opinion about her home. It sounds like a big job."

Knox had a sinking suspicion he knew who Liv was talking about. "Penelope Duvall?"

Liv nodded, a big smile on her face. "Do you know her?"

Lifting his eyebrows, Knox asked, "Do you?"

Her smile slipped just a little, and she crinkled her nose. "That bad, huh?"

Knox lifted his hands and shook his head. "I'm not saying anything."

"Okay." Liv laughed. "I can handle myself. I work with all sorts of different people."

Merritt listened to their conversation, and Knox couldn't ignore the look on her face. She wore her emotions openly and was easy to read. He knew she didn't like Penelope, even though they had not spoken about her since the night they'd gone to her house for supper. But he wasn't blind. He knew Merritt and Penelope had not gotten along, and he suspected something had happened between them, though Merritt never said a word.

He smiled at her, hoping to reassure her, and tenderly laid his hand on the small of her back to stay close to her in the crush of people.

She glanced up at him, a gentle smile on her lips.

His heart leaped at the sight, and his affection for her grew even stronger.

Slowly, he removed his hand, afraid he was losing all ability to control his heart.

Chapter Nine

Merritt wiped the sweat from her brow as she stood and surveyed the work she'd just done on the girls' playhouse.

"What do you think?" Knox asked her as he set down the two-by-fours he had hauled from the driveway to the work site.

"It's going to be amazing," Merritt said. "I'm shocked at how quickly it's coming together."

"Having Matt's construction crew here has made all the difference." Knox wiped his hands on his worn jeans. "I'm just thankful they had an opening this week. The electrician will be here in the morning to run wires for the lights and outlets. Then we'll get it insulated and put up the drywall next week. After the frame is up, Matt's crew will roof it and side it. He thinks the shell will be done by the end of next week."

Merritt could only watch the crew of four men in awe. They worked in perfect unison, hardly talking as they each did their jobs. Thankfully, they had been patient and accommodating enough to allow Merritt to help and had given her the job of screwing the bolts on the bottom of the walls to the concrete pad underneath.

It was hot and humid, but here, under the shade of the pine trees, with a gentle breeze blowing off the lake, it was pleasant. She longed to jump into the lake to cool off even more but knew that at the end of the day, when everyone left, they'd have the whole evening to enjoy.

After being at Knox's place for two weeks, Merritt felt like she'd been there her whole life. They'd found a gentle rhythm to their days: early-morning chores and breakfast, followed by work on the playhouse, then cooking supper together, playing with the girls in the lake or the yard, and then a quiet evening on the patio with a fire to watch the sunset and talk.

It was exactly what Merritt needed to ease the ache in her heart over her failed engagement. She'd already learned so much about herself and realized a lot about her relationship with Brad. Though she was still hurt, she had found a way to forgive him and wish him well in his new marriage.

The foreman called everyone to stop for lunch, and Merritt looked at Knox. "Are you hungry?"

"Ravenous." He grinned.

"How about we stop for lunch, too?"

They left the men at the work site and walked across the lawn toward the house. The girls had been invited to spend the day with Veronica and Penelope at the local zoo and had left early that morning. It had made working on the playhouse a little easier, since they didn't need to keep an eye on the girls or make sure they were entertained.

Knox opened the back door, and Darby came bounding out to do her business. Merritt entered the air-conditioned kitchen, finding immediate relief from the heat and humidity.

"I must look like a mess," she said, keenly aware of the sweat and grime all over her skin. She was wearing a pair of faded shorts and an old T-shirt. Sawdust clung to her hair and clothes.

"You look great," Knox said with a smile. "Hard work looks good on everyone."

She looked him over and had to agree. He was just as sweaty and grimy, with twice the sawdust covering him since he had been cutting most of the lumber, but he still looked as handsome as ever. She'd been surprised to learn that he had worked for a construction company during his high school and college breaks. It now made sense that he was so confident about such a big construction project.

There was something very appealing about a man who knew how to build something with his hands. And to know that Knox not only built it, but also designed it, was pretty impressive.

"How do sandwiches sound?" Knox asked as he opened the refrigerator door, oblivious to her wayward thoughts.

"Sandwiches sound great." Merritt went to the sink to wash her hands, forcing herself to stop thinking about Knox—if that was possible.

They were in the middle of constructing their sandwiches, working in companionable silence, when Merritt's phone dinged with a message. She ignored it and finished making her meal. They decided to eat indoors at the counter to stay cool for as long as possible, and when Merritt took a seat on her stool, she had to pull her phone out of her back pocket to sit down.

That's when she saw whom the message was from.

She went still as she lifted the phone and pressed the buttons necessary to open the email.

Knox glanced at her as he poured two glasses of lemonade and brought one to her.

"Everything okay?" he asked.

Merritt swallowed, not sure how to answer. It was better than okay.

"It's from one of the schools I applied to in James Island. Oakhill Academy. My dream job at one of the most exclusive private schools in the Charleston area. They have an opening for a kindergarten teacher, but it's almost impossible to even get an interview with them—let alone a position." She quickly read the email, her heart pounding and her hands trembling, unable to believe what she was seeing. "They'd like to interview me next week. I'm one of three candidates they're considering, but with my connection to James Island and my résumé, they're very hopeful that I will be a good fit for the school."

Merritt looked up at Knox. The expression on his face was a mixture of joy and sadness.

"That's amazing, Merritt. I'm very happy for you. I hope you get the job, if that's what you want."

"It's what I've always wanted. Most of the teachers who work there stay until they retire—that's why it's so difficult to get in. I'd be set for life."

Her sandwich was all but forgotten as she pressed the reply button to tell the principal she'd love to be interviewed. But then stopped. Would she need to fly home for the interview? And if she flew home, what would be the point in coming back? Knox was doing an amazing job with the girls. He didn't really need her anymore. He was a natural with them.

"If I interview for this job," she said, hesitantly, "I will need to return to Charleston—but I've committed to staying here for the summer."

"You need to interview, Merritt. This is a once-in-a-lifetime opportunity for you."

For some reason, she was disappointed that he didn't tell her to stay. But why would he?

"Will you come back?" he asked quietly, his sandwich sitting on his plate, untouched.

She couldn't look at him—didn't want to see the emotions in his eyes and try to guess what they meant.

"I don't know." She frowned, looking at the email but not reading it. "Is there a reason for me to come back?"

"I thought we had more time."

"That's not a reason."

"What about the girls' party? And the playhouse? They'll be crushed if you're not here to celebrate with them."

She bit her bottom lip as she thought about the future and the distance between Minnesota and South Carolina. "I can't be here for all the parties and milestones over the years."

"I hope you can be here for some of them."

Merritt still couldn't look at him, afraid she might cry. She didn't want to think about missing the important moments in Blair's and Addison's lives.

"They have their hopes set on this party," Knox said gently. "I'd be happy to pay for your ticket to come back—even if it's just for a few days, though I hope it can be for longer."

Merritt's phone dinged again, and this time it was a text from Joy Asher.

Thankful for a little distraction from this weighty discussion, Merritt tapped on the message and read it, her breath catching at the words on the screen.

"Joy took it upon herself to tell the Timber Falls Christian school about me. They've asked for my résumé and want to set up a time for an interview in the next couple of weeks."

Knox didn't speak, so Merritt finally looked at him. He was studying her closely.

"Do you have any desire to stay and teach in Timber Falls?" he finally asked. "Because if not, please don't feel obligated to send them your résumé. The last thing I'd want is for you to do it out of guilt—and possibly give up your dream job."

Merritt swallowed, her breath feeling shallow. "I don't know what I want anymore. I love the girls and I'm quickly falling in love with Timber Falls—and this lake." *And you*, she wanted to add, though she didn't dare. She couldn't be in love with him. She had only really known him for two weeks—and the years she'd known *of* him before that, she'd been all wrong about him. "It would be foolish of me not to put in my résumé at the Timber Falls Christian school. The job in James Island might not pan out. I need to have options, don't I?"

"Then you'll need to come back here for the interview, won't you?" Knox asked.

The hope in his voice made her smile. "I will."

"And you'll be able to stay for the party, right?"

"Are you sure you want me to come back, Knox?"

"Of course I do."

She wished she could ask him if he wanted her back for the girls' sake—or for his. But she couldn't. There was no reason to know. She had a lot of decisions to make, and she didn't need anything to complicate those choices.

"You don't need to head back before the Fourth of July, do you?" he asked. "I was really looking forward to celebrating with you."

"My interview is July seventh, so I can leave after the Fourth. My parents are still in Europe, but I can stay at their house. I'll plan on coming back to Minnesota the following week. That'll give us a few more weeks until the girls' party to plan and work on the playhouse. Do you think you'll be okay with the girls for a week alone?"

Knox nodded. "It won't be the same, but we'll manage."

Merritt felt a measure of relief, knowing that at least one difficult decision had been made for her. She had a reason to come back to Timber Falls.

Ever since Merritt's email from the school in South Carolina four days ago, things had been different between her and Knox—and he didn't like it. She was a lot more distracted, and not in a good way. He would have expected her to be overjoyed at the prospect of interviewing for her dream job—yet she was more impatient and preoccupied than he'd ever seen her.

But he understood she had been through a lot the past month, and she had some big decisions to make. All her plans had been in upheaval since her wedding had been canceled, and she needed time and space to figure things out. If she was a little impatient or pre-occupied lately, it was understandable.

Knox filled a picnic basket with the fried chicken he'd made earlier and the potato salad the girls liked so much. Merritt had taken Blair and Addison upstairs, putting on sweatshirts to go out on the lake for a late supper picnic and fireworks. It was the Fourth of July, and Merritt would be leaving bright and early the next morning to drive to the Minneapolis airport. It was about a hundred miles, and her flight left at noon. She'd use Knox's SUV and park it at the airport and then bring it back next week when she returned. He had a Jeep he only used in the summer and wouldn't miss the SUV.

"We're ready!" Addy called as she skipped into the kitchen, Blair on her heels. "Have the fireworks started yet?"

"Not until dusk," Knox said as he filled a cooler with some soda pop as a treat for the girls.

Merritt came in next, wearing a pair of cropped jeans, a plain white T-shirt, tucked in at the front, and a pair of sandals. She had a cardigan over her arm and wore her hair loose tonight. It was long and flowed down to the middle of her back. Her dimples popped out when she caught his gaze and offered a sad smile.

Was she as unhappy to leave as he was to see her go? It would be so strange without her in the house for the next week.

"Do you need help with anything?" she asked him.

"I think I have everything ready. I could use some help carrying out the picnic basket."

She closed the lid and lifted it while Knox picked up the cooler.

"Can Darby come with us?" Addy asked. "She likes the pontoon."

"Sure she can come." Knox opened the back door. "Hopefully she's not scared of fireworks."

"She won't be scared," Blair said. "She loves fireworks."

"How do you know?" Knox asked.

"We watched the fireworks with Mrs. Masterson last year. Darby barked the whole time."

Knox glanced at Merritt, leery with the idea of taking the dog if she was going to be upset.

"Mrs. Masterson had to put her in the house," Addy said. "And she barked inside, too."

"See?" Blair said. "She's not scared of them."

"Well," Knox said with a sigh, "we'll see how she does."

The little troop walked onto the patio, toward the lake.

"Yoo-hoo!" Penelope called out from her yard.

Knox wished he could have ignored her, but she and Veronica started to walk toward them.

"Hi, Ronnie!" Addison called out to her friend. "Are you ready?"

"Ready?" Knox asked.

"Ronnie and her mom are coming with us," Blair said. "Can they, Daddy?"

Merritt's shoulders tightened, and she stopped walking as she looked in Penelope's direction. Knox could see the mistrust in her eyes.

"We didn't know what to bring," Penelope called, still walking toward them with a large bag in hand. "The girls said you'd have supper for us, but I wanted to bring something, so I had my cook make a couple of desserts. Thank you so much for the invitation.

We weren't sure how we were going to celebrate the Fourth of July."

"I think I'll stay behind," Merritt said to Knox. "Give you more room on the pontoon."

"No." Knox shook his head. He wasn't going to give up this last evening with Merritt without a fight. Penelope was still far enough away she couldn't hear their exchange.

"I have stuff I need to do," Merritt said, handing Knox the picnic basket. "I'll be fine."

"Please," he said. "Don't stay home. I want you to come."

"I didn't know Penelope was coming."

"I didn't, either," he whispered. "The girls must have invited her." He pleaded with his eyes. "Merritt, I want you to come. I've been looking forward to this evening all week."

She studied him, her gaze hooded.

"Thank you for waiting for us," Penelope said, oblivious to the tension she'd created. She took the picnic basket from Knox's hand and didn't acknowledge Merritt. "All Veronica could talk about this week was the picnic on the lake and the fireworks. Your girls have made it sound amazing."

Knox couldn't possibly tell Penelope and Veronica that they weren't welcome. It would be cruel to the girls.

Merritt seemed to realize the same thing, because she lifted her chin and put a smile on her lips. She directed her comment to Veronica and the twins. "Do you know when fireworks were invented?"

She walked with the girls toward the lake, leaving

Knox back with Penelope, who made no move to follow them.

"This was such a nice gesture," Penelope said, putting her free hand on Knox's bicep.

His muscles clenched beneath her touch.

"I've been longing to spend more time with you," she continued. "*Alone.* Hopefully we can make that happen later."

Merritt glanced back, her gaze landing on Penelope's hand.

"I don't think tonight will be a good night." Knox moved away from her touch and started walking toward the lake.

It took a while to get settled into the large pontoon. Darby sat near the front while the girls sat around the table in the back, their pop cans already opened as they giggled and talked incessantly.

Knox lowered the electric boat lift and the pontoon began to float, then he turned on the engine and slowly moved it away from the dock. Penelope took the seat next to him, while Merritt sat behind him, across from the girls. From where Knox sat, he could only see Merritt in the small rearview mirror. She looked pensive and quiet as she watched the lake. The wind blew her hair in a dark cloud of silk. He didn't think it was possible, but she had become more and more beautiful to him every day.

"You're quiet," Penelope said to Knox, pulling his gaze away from Merritt.

He pressed his lips together and tried to smile, but it fell flat.

They rode out to the middle of the lake, where they'd have the best view of all the fireworks displays. There were dozens of other boats already out there, neighbors and friends Knox had known most of his life, tethering their boats and pontoons together. He turned off the engine and put down the anchor, then he turned to the ladies in his boat and said, "Who's hungry?"

An hour later, the sun had dipped behind the horizon, everyone's bellies were full and Knox sat on the back bench, next to Merritt. Penelope had gone to the front of the pontoon as she talked with a neighboring boat of men, younger than her but no less interested in the flashy woman.

The girls were on their knees, their elbows on the lip of the pontoon, watching the fireworks. And, surprisingly, Darby had fallen asleep by Knox's feet. Out on the lake, the fireworks weren't as loud as they'd be on land and didn't seem to bother her.

Merritt was close, so close he could smell the floral scent of her shampoo. He wanted to reach out and touch her hair, her hand, her cheek. But he refrained.

"I'm going to miss you," he said instead.

She was quiet for a moment, but then she turned and looked at him. "I'm going to miss you, too."

He wanted to tell her that he didn't want her to go, that he wanted her to stay and be a part of their lives for good. But it was purely selfish of him. He wasn't prepared to offer her his heart or the promise of a life together, but he also wasn't ready to let her go forever. He wanted more time to figure out what was happening between them—and if he could trust himself to make such a big decision again. What would happen if he asked her to stay, only to realize that they weren't compatible for the long term? Or that he wasn't ready to settle down? He still had a job that required him to be gone for weeks and months out of the year. Could a relationship last with those kinds of separations? He'd rather have her platonic friendship than nothing at all.

But, more importantly, he didn't know how she felt about him. There were days when he thought that maybe she was growing to care for him, but then she'd remind him that he wasn't the type of man she was attracted to, or he'd realize her affection for him was connected to the girls. And then he'd second-guess her feelings.

"Do you have everything you need?" he asked.

She just smiled at him. Of course she did.

"Are you sure you don't want me to drive you to the airport?" He wished she'd let him.

"It would cut into your day." She shook her head. "If you're okay with me parking the SUV there for the week, then I don't see the need for you to drive me."

"I'm okay with whatever you want." He would do anything she asked him to do. "And you set up your interview at Timber Falls Community Christian School?"

"Yes. It's not until the twenty-first of this month."

"Good." He wanted reassurance that she'd come back as planned.

"Knox?" she asked.

"Yes?"

"Thank you." She smiled, and her dimples almost undid his resolve not to ask her to stay. "For welcoming me into your family and for being such a great guy."

He did take her hand then and held it tenderly for a moment before letting her go.

Chapter Ten

It had been the longest ten days of Merritt's life. What should have only been a weeklong trip back to South Carolina had been extended because of a broken water pipe at her parents' house. And since they were still in Europe, they'd asked Merritt if she could postpone her return to Minnesota to make sure everything was handled properly.

Now, as she stepped out of Knox's SUV in his driveway, she took a deep breath. It was late—later than she would have liked. The stars were vibrant overhead, and the wind was whispering in the height of the pine trees. A single light had been left on in the entryway, which Knox had probably done for Merritt. She had texted him right before leaving the airport to tell him she was on her way back. She hadn't wanted to open the garage door, afraid it might wake up the girls.

Just seeing the house again filled her with a sense of warmth and peace. Not only because of the people inside, but because she'd fallen in love with Minnesota—and especially this lake and home. She couldn't wait to see what had been accomplished on the playhouse.

After retrieving her small carry-on bag, she walked up to the front door and found it unlocked.

Her heart pounded, wondering if she'd see Knox tonight or if he'd already gone to bed.

As quietly as possible, she entered the house and locked the door behind her. The sound of a television caught her ear first, and then she noticed a soft blue light coming from the great room. Had Knox stayed awake?

Anticipation raced up her spine. They'd spoken a few times while she was gone, but it hadn't been the same as seeing him face-to-face. She missed him and the girls dearly, and it had only been ten days. What would it be like when she was gone for good?

Merritt set her bag and keys in the entry and walked down the hall to the great room on the right.

The Little Mermaid was playing on the television, and Knox was sitting on the floor with his back against the sofa. The girls were on either side of him, having fallen asleep with their heads on his lap. He had one hand on Blair's back and one on Addison's—but it was his hair that made Merritt pause and grin.

It was clear he had let the girls style his hair. There were dozens of barrettes, clips, ponytails and head-bands on his head. It also looked like they'd had a carpet picnic of treats. There was a bag of chips, a container of cookies and a bowl of popcorn next to the girls' cups, which looked like they were half-full of chocolate milk.

Knox turned at the sound of Merritt's entrance, and his face filled with the most beautiful smile she'd ever seen in her life. His eyes lit up with joy. "Merritt. You're home."

Home.

It didn't matter that he looked silly. He had never been more attractive or appealing to her. And in that moment, Merritt knew she had lost her heart. She could no longer deny the truth, though she would never admit it to anyone.

He started to get up, but she lifted her hand to stop him. Instead, she came into the room and squatted down next to Blair, close to Knox.

"Welcome back," he said quietly, his smile still as bright as it had been when she entered.

It took all her willpower not to reach out and touch him. Her hands ached to trace the lines of his cheeks, to touch his smile and feel the gentleness of his lips.

But it was a futile desire. So much had changed since she'd been away.

"It looks like you had a fun evening," she said, glancing at the leftovers.

"They don't get treats often," he said, "and they were so excited that you were coming back. They begged me to let them stay awake until you got here. I said they could give it a try, but they both fell asleep about an hour ago."

"And you kept watching *The Little Mermaid*?"

He laughed and shook his head. "I was trapped and didn't want to move either one. Besides—" He shrugged. "It's been a while since I saw it, and it still holds my interest all these years later."

"Would you like me to help move them to bed?" She was still talking quietly so she wouldn't disturb them.

"Sure."

Merritt reached for Blair. She was getting so big, but not big enough that Merritt couldn't carry her.

Blair moaned and scrunched up her face.

"It's okay, Blair-bear," Merritt said to the little girl, bringing her close and holding her tenderly. "It's Auntie Merritt."

Blair's eyes opened, and they were glossy as she looked at Merritt. She tried to smile, but she grimaced. "I don't feel good," she said.

"I'm not surprised." Merritt glanced at the junk food on the coffee table again. "It looks like you had some yummy food tonight. But it probably didn't sit well on your tummy."

Blair wrapped her arm around Merritt's neck, pressing her cheek to Merritt's. Her skin was hot to the touch.

"It feels like she might have a fever," Merritt said to Knox as she watched him pick up Addison. The little girl wrapped her legs around Knox's waist and looked at Merritt.

She grinned. "Auntie Merritt!"

"Hello, sweetie," Merritt said to Addison as she leaned over and kissed the girl's cheek.

"Blair has a fever?" Knox asked, his eyebrows dipping in concern.

"And she says she doesn't feel good."

Guilt washed over Knox's face. "I probably shouldn't have let them eat all this junk."

"A few treats now and again aren't going to hurt them," Merritt said. "If she's running a fever, I don't think it's from the cookies and chips."

Knox reached out and placed his hand on Blair's forehead. She moaned and moved away from his touch.

"Where does it hurt?" Merritt asked her.

"My tummy," Blair said.

Merritt met Knox's gaze. "What do you think we should do?"

He looked like he was at a loss. "I have no experience with stuff like this."

"Kids get sick in my classroom all the time," Merritt assured him. "I think we should give her some Tylenol and monitor her to see if she has any other symptoms. It might just be a stomach bug."

"They have been spending a lot of time with Penelope and Veronica this past week," Knox said. "They've been all over the area to amusement parks, beaches, waterparks, shopping—she could have easily picked up something."

Merritt tried not to let her disappointment in hearing about Penelope show. She had wondered if Knox would see Penelope while she was gone—but had tried not to think about it often.

"Blair," Merritt said to her niece, "I'm going to give you some medicine to help make you feel better, okay?"

Blair nodded but didn't lift her head off Merritt's shoulder.

Twenty minutes later, after putting the girls to bed and giving Blair a bucket in case she needed to use it during the night, Merritt and Knox left the girls' room and stood out in the dark hall.

"Thanks for coming back," Knox said. "I don't know what I would have done if you weren't here tonight. You always know how to handle each situation."

"You would have figured it out." Merritt smiled at him. "You're a lot better at this parenting thing than you think."

He leaned against the wall and shook his head, the hair clips, headbands and ponytails looking as ridiculous—

and endearing—as before. "What you don't know is that I called my mom at least a dozen times while you were gone to ask for her advice."

"Why didn't you call me?"

"I didn't want you to know how inept I was."

Merritt couldn't stop smiling as she shook her head. A yawn escaped her mouth, and she covered it with her hand. It had been a long day of traveling.

"I shouldn't keep you awake," he said.

"It's okay."

"I'm just happy you're back, Merritt."

"So am I."

"How did your interview go?"

Merritt pressed her lips together, unsure if she wanted to talk about it now. There was so much to say—so much she still needed to sort out.

"It went really, really well."

His smile was still present, but it dimmed a little. He tried to bolster it, though. "That's great. Did they offer you the job?"

"Not yet—but I think they will. They said they hope to let me know early next week. I was their first candidate to interview."

"Wow." He nodded but didn't say anything else.

"If I get the job, I'll need to leave the day after the girls' birthday so I have time to set up my classroom before the school year starts."

The girls' birthday was on August fifth. Three weeks from today. It sounded like a long time, but it didn't feel like a long time. Not when it meant that she would be saying goodbye to Knox and the girls.

"Are you still going to interview with the Timber Falls school?" he asked.

"I might hear from Oakhill before that." She lifted her shoulders. "I don't plan to cancel my interview with Timber Falls unless I get the job in James Island."

Knox nodded slowly as he stood straight and offered her a sad smile. "I guess we'll just have to wait and see what happens."

"I guess."

"Good night, Merritt."

"Good night, Knox."

He lifted his hand—and then hesitated a moment before touching her cheek.

She put her hand over his, loving the feel of his skin against hers.

And then he dropped his hand and walked down the hall to his room, leaving Merritt to wrestle with her emotions.

It was dark when Knox opened his eyes. He lay in his bed for a minute, wondering what had woken him up. A quick glance at his alarm clock told him it was only two in the morning.

He turned to his other side and looked out the window toward the inky blackness of night, his heart still heavy from his conversation with Merritt. Part of him had hoped that things didn't go well at Oakhill—but that was the selfish part. If it was her dream job, and it was the thing that would make her happy, then he wanted it for her, even if it meant saying goodbye.

Forcing the thoughts aside, he focused, instead, on how much he had missed her and how happy he'd been when she walked into the great room a few hours ago. He had completely forgotten about his hair until he'd come back to his room—and couldn't do anything but laugh as he took the clips and headbands off his head.

There had been an emptiness in him the past ten days—an emptiness that Merritt had filled the moment she had walked back into his home. How was he going to let her go in just three short weeks? He'd heard from Mrs. Masterson, and she said she hoped to be back by the girls' birthday. Her daughter was doing well in physical therapy and should be able to be on her own in two or three weeks.

Did that mean that things would go back to normal?

Knox placed his hand over his heart as he continued to look out the windows. How would things return to normal? He could never leave the girls for as long as he had before—and he didn't want to. Everything was different now, and he'd be foolish to think it wasn't.

A strange sound filtered through the door, causing Knox to frown. It almost sounded like someone was crying.

He sat up, wondering if the sound had been the thing to awaken him.

Darby was soon at Knox's door, scratching and whining, so he got out of bed and pulled on a T-shirt and then tightened the drawstring on his pajama bottoms.

Someone was definitely crying.

He opened his bedroom door and petted Darby's head, his pulse starting to escalate. The crying was coming from the girls' bedroom.

Knox didn't waste another moment. He sprinted down the hall and opened the girls' bedroom door.

Blair had kicked her blankets off and was curled

up in a ball, crying. Addison looked like she had just woken up, confused, as she blinked and frowned.

"Blair." Knox rushed to her side. "What's wrong, sweetheart?"

"My tummy," Blair said without opening her eyes. "It hurts." Her cheeks were wet from her tears, and when Knox put his hand on her forehead, it was burning up.

Merritt appeared at the girls' door just then, wrapping a cardigan around her waist. "What's wrong?"

"She's in a lot of pain." Knox pushed Blair's hair off her cheeks. "She says it's her stomach."

Addison started to cry then, too. "Is Blairy going to die?"

"No." Merritt shook her head as she knelt between the two beds and put her hand on Blair's forehead, just like Knox had done. "Blair, can I touch your tummy?"

Blair shook her head. "It hurts."

"I need to see if it's tender," she said. "It's very important."

Blair let Merritt turn her so she could touch her stomach, but the moment Merritt laid her hand on the right side of Blair's midsection, she cried out in pain and clenched into a ball again.

"I think it's her appendix," Merritt said to Knox. "Even if it's not, we should get her to the hospital."

Knox sat back on his heels, panic and guilt falling upon him with force. Why hadn't he taken Blair's complaints before bed more seriously? What if they were too late?

Merritt went into action, grabbing a couple outfits from the girls' closet and stuffing them into a bag. She found Blair's favorite blanket and teddy bear and put them in the bag, too.

It didn't take long for Knox to pull himself together. He lifted Blair off the bed, despite her protests and cries of pain, and walked her to the hallway. Merritt followed with Addison, who clung to her tight, her blue eyes big with worry. Though he didn't know what Merritt was telling Addison, he could hear her speaking soothing words.

In a few minutes, they were in the SUV. Merritt sat in the back, between the two girls, comforting both of them. She laid Blair's blanket over her and asked Addison to hold on to Blair's teddy bear for her sister.

It took them twenty minutes to get to the hospital, and Knox was so thankful he had Merritt's help. He wouldn't have been able to do it without her. While he dealt with registering Blair, Merritt rocked her in her arms and whispered reassuring words to both the girls until the nurse came out to the waiting room to get them.

The four of them went into the back of the ER, and everything was a blur from there. Knox was grateful they were in such good hands—even as he sat back feeling helpless.

"We're going to need to take her into emergency surgery," Dr. Epley said to Knox. "It's her appendix, and it needs to come out as soon as possible."

"Yes, of course," Knox said. "Do whatever you need to do."

As the doctor quickly explained the procedure and what to expect, Knox just stood there, trying desperately to absorb everything he was being told. He looked at Merritt, who was nodding, and he hoped she was remembering everything, because he felt so overwhelmed. All he could do was hold Blair's hand as the doctor talked.

Before long, they were kissing Blair and telling her everything would be all right. They had just a moment to pray for her, and then she was wheeled down the bright hallway, through the wide double doors. She looked so little and afraid, clutching her teddy bear in one arm. Knox walked with her until they reached the doors and the nurse told him he could go no farther.

Addison was crying in Merritt's arms when Knox turned back.

Merritt's eyes were soft with concern as she studied him. Guilt still weighed heavy on Knox's shoulders. The doctor wasn't sure if the appendix had already ruptured, but if it had, Blair might be looking at a long stay in the hospital and a strong antibiotic treatment. Even if it hadn't ruptured, she'd probably be in the hospital for a few days. He couldn't imagine the pain or fear his daughter was feeling.

"It's not your fault, Knox," Merritt said to him, watching him closely.

How did she know him so well?

"I should have brought her in last night," he told her.

"There was no way you could have known."

"I don't know what I would have done without you." He shook his head. "What if this had happened when you were still gone? You and Mrs. Masterson are so much better equipped to parent than I am. What if something like this happens again and I'm the only one here?" The reality of the situation washed over him, sucking the air from his lungs. He wasn't capable of caring for his daughters on his own.

"You would have known what to do, even if I wasn't here." Her words were meant to console him, but they didn't offer any reassurance. He was in over his head.

Merritt reached out her hand, and he did the only thing he could think to do—the natural thing. He wrapped Merritt and Addy in his embrace.

The three of them stood in the middle of the ER hallway, holding each other, praying that everything would turn out okay.

Chapter Eleven

The hospital was quiet as Merritt sat next to Addison on the sofa in the family waiting room. Thankfully, the little girl had fallen back to sleep, but her tearstained face was still scrunched up in worry. Merritt ran her hand over Addy's forehead, trying to offer comfort, even while she slept. The bond the twin sisters shared was unlike anything Merritt had ever witnessed. Blair's pain had become Addy's, and the little girl had been suffering almost as much as her sister until she drifted off to sleep.

Knox had been restless since a nurse had shown them into the waiting room. He was on his feet, a disposable coffee cup in hand, pacing from one side of the room to the other. The clock said it was after four, but the large plate-glass windows on the outside wall revealed a dark and starless night beyond. Most of the lights in the waiting room were off, allowing Addy to sleep, but a faint glow came through the door facing the hall. A large fish aquarium sat in the middle of the room, dividing it into two sections and offering a little more light, allowing Merritt to watch Knox.

He hadn't spoken much since Blair had been wheeled into surgery, and though Merritt had tried to reassure him, she suspected he still felt guilty about what had happened with his daughter. It wasn't his fault, or anyone else's.

Merritt slowly stood and readjusted Addy until she was sleeping peacefully again under Blair's blanket, then walked across the room to join Knox.

He stopped pacing near the fish tank and stared at the colorful inhabitants swimming gently within.

"How are you doing?" Merritt asked quietly.

Knox glanced up and met her gaze. There were so many emotions floating within his eyes, weighing down his countenance. "How could I have let this happen?"

Merritt frowned. "You didn't let this happen, Knox."

"I shouldn't have let her eat all that junk food tonight. She was feeling fine before—"

"This has nothing to do with what she ate tonight. Her appendix would have become infected regardless. You know that."

He sighed and looked down at his coffee cup, absently swishing the liquid around before setting it on a table. "You're right." He shook his head and ran his hands through his hair in frustration. "My guilt isn't just about tonight, but it feels like the final straw. I've been such a failure to my girls, Merritt, and this just proves it all over again."

"A failure?" Merritt couldn't believe what she was hearing. "You're far from a failure, Knox. You've given them an amazing life."

"Everything I've offered them is material." He finally looked up at her, his face filled with regret and pain. "When they needed me most, I abandoned them. And my greatest fear is that one day soon, they're going to realize the truth. I'm just thankful I was here tonight to be with Blair and Addy."

"Knox, what you went through with Reina was devastating." She swallowed the misgivings she felt speaking about her sister. "I know you made a lot of decisions that brought you to this moment, but Reina is the one who abandoned those girls. You were reeling and trying to figure out your new normal." All the built-up anger and resentment Merritt had harbored for her sister came to the forefront of her emotions, and her voice shook. "I've known Reina my whole life, and not once did she do something sacrificial for anyone else. Time and time again, she hurt the people closest to her. Maybe you shouldn't have left the girls for such long periods of time—but I know you would have been a different father and husband if given the chance."

He studied her, his blue eyes so soft and yet so intense. "In all the ways she hurt the girls and me," he said quietly, "I never stopped to think about how she must have hurt you, too."

"Do you want to know the truth?" Merritt bit her bottom lip for a moment to stop the trembling. "Knowing how she treated you and the girls hurts far more than anything she ever did to me. I don't know how she could have left you."

"I don't know how Brad could have left you, either."

They stared at one another for a heartbeat, and Merritt knew that if she leaned close to him, he would take her into his arms. The pull between them was strong and impossible to ignore, and they were both yearning for comfort in that moment.

But she also knew that she was exhausted and that both of them were emotionally drained. Not just from the course of events that had unfolded tonight, but from weeks of uncertainty preceding this moment. If she gave in to the pull, she would regret her actions. And she knew he would, too.

She had some big decisions to make over the next few weeks, and she didn't need any more complications to confuse matters.

"Would you like more coffee?" Merritt asked, her eyes feeling gritty from lack of sleep. She had been exhausted coming in from Charleston and had only been asleep for about an hour when Blair's cries had woken her up. "I could use some."

Knox watched her quietly, questions in his eyes. Had he wanted her to respond to his statement? Had he been hoping she would have leaned into him?

Instead of asking, he straightened his shoulders, concern etched between his brows. "I didn't stop to think about how tired you are. I should have offered to get *you* some coffee."

"It's okay. You've been a little preoccupied. I don't mind getting it."

The coffee machine was in the corner of the room on a counter that held tea and hot chocolate packets, as well. Merritt picked up Knox's cold coffee and brought it to the counter to dump it down the sink. She tossed away the cup before taking two fresh ones off the stack.

Knox followed her.

There was a soft light on over the coffee bar, allowing Merritt to see what she was doing—but having him standing so close to her made her feel clumsy and unsure of herself.

"Have you spoken to Reina lately?" His voice was gentle—tentative.

Merritt licked her dry lips as she continued to work on the coffee. Did he really want to know? And, if he did, would it matter? He hadn't asked about her before now.

"The last time I heard from Reina was briefly at Christmas." She put the cup under the spout of the machine and pressed the appropriate button. "She's living in California, working as a personal trainer in LA. She name-dropped several celebrities she's working with right now."

"Do you think she's happy?"

Happy? It was hard to tell if Reina had ever been happy. She never revealed her emotions to anyone. Though she was fun and outgoing, no one ever really saw inside Reina's heart or mind. "As happy as she can be." Merritt stared at the cup as the machine began to pour out the coffee.

"Do you know how to get ahold of her?"

Merritt finally turned to look at him, her eyebrows drawn together. "Do you really want to know?"

"No matter what she did to me, she's still the girls' mother. I think I should call her and tell her what's happening to Blair."

Something caught in Merritt's heart at his words, and in that moment, she realized she didn't think Reina deserved to know. Reina had not once made an effort to even ask whether or not Merritt or her parents knew anything about Blair and Addison. In the very rare moments they had spoken in the past four and a half years, she had not brought up their names at all.

She had only talked about herself. It was as if they had never existed to her.

"Do you think she would want to know?" Merritt asked him.

"I think—at least I hope—in her heart of hearts, she does. Maybe she doesn't know how to reach out."

A sense of unease rippled inside Merritt. What if Knox and Reina reconnected and he fell for her all over again? What if she became a part of the girls' lives, only to hurt them? It was none of Merritt's business whether or not Knox reached out to her, but she wanted to spare them the pain.

Actually, if she was being honest with herself, she wanted to spare herself the pain, as well. She couldn't sit back and watch Reina manipulate and hurt Knox and the girls again.

"I want to at least give her the option of knowing," Knox said.

It wasn't Merritt's place to make a decision about Reina. That decision belonged to Knox. "I have her cell phone number," Merritt said, trying not to let her true feelings show. "I hardly ever use it. I don't even know if it's the right number anymore."

The machine stopped, and Merritt removed the cup, then set it on the counter and put the next cup in place. After the coffee was pouring again, she took her cell phone out of her back pocket and went to her contacts list. Her fingers were trembling as she searched for Reina's name.

Knox stood, motionless, as Merritt tapped a few buttons and texted him Reina's contact information.

A second later, Knox's phone dinged, but he didn't

pull it out. He just studied Merritt. "Thank you. I know it's not easy for you to talk about her."

She slipped her phone back into her pocket, a dozen emotions flooding her senses. Would she regret sending that text to him? "I hope she cares. I really do."

"So do I."

Merritt could tell he truly meant what he was saying.

Knox stared at the number Merritt had sent him as he sat in the quiet waiting room, hoping to hear from the doctor soon. It was too late to call Reina tonight. The time difference in California meant it was just after two in the morning there. Yet, now that he had the number, that's all he could think about. He had told himself he'd never talk to Reina again, but something had shifted inside him tonight as he'd watched Blair being wheeled into surgery.

Merritt sat next to Addy on the sofa, her hand on the little girl's back as she leaned her head against the wall and closed her eyes. He hoped she would get some rest, but he had a sneaking suspicion she wasn't sleeping.

Something had passed between them earlier, but he was too tired and too overwhelmed to put his finger on exactly what it had been. They hadn't had much time to talk about her interview this past week, though he knew it had gone well and she was expecting Oakhill Academy to make an offer. But where did that leave them? She deserved so much more than what he could offer right now. All he could tell her was that he adored her and thought the world of her. That if things had been different, there might have been a chance for them. Yet, things were not different. She was Reina's sister and the girls' aunt. And, if that wasn't enough, he was still uncertain of happily-ever-afters. Too many things could go wrong, and the last person he wanted to hurt was Merritt. He cared about her too much to break her heart.

Besides, he still had a job that would call him away to Spain in September, and he would be gone for several weeks. There was the possibility that he could pass his traveling responsibilities to one of his team members, but he had always enjoyed being on the go. Would all that change now? He couldn't imagine not being here for Blair or Addy at a time like this.

Knox stood, his heart heavy and his thoughts too jumbled to stay in one place. He needed to move.

Merritt opened her eyes. "Is something wrong?"

"I just need to keep moving. I hate this waiting."

"Hopefully it won't be much longer."

He nodded. "Do you mind staying with Addy if I walk the halls a little bit?"

"I don't mind." Her voice was soft and gentle, and her eyes were full of compassion. She had always offered him the utmost respect and understanding, even when he'd asked her for Reina's number. He could see how much it had troubled her, but she had still given it to him, trusting him to make the right decision.

He just wished he was worthy of her confidence.

Knox left the waiting room, his phone heavy in his pocket. All he could think about right now was calling Reina, even though it was two in the morning in California. If he left a voice message and tossed the ball into her court, maybe she'd call him back—or maybe she wouldn't. But if he did call her, then maybe this strange pressure he felt in his chest would ease up a bit.

Without allowing himself another moment of indecision, he pulled his phone out of his pocket and tapped the number on the screen.

The phone began to ring, and each time it did, his nerves eased more and more. She wouldn't answer and he could simply leave a message. It would be so much easier than talking to her in person.

"Hello?" A feminine voice picked up on the other end.

Knox paused midstride in the hallway, his heart thumping wildly in his chest. "Reina?"

"Who is this?"

He swallowed the lump in his throat and let out a breath, hoping and praying he could get through this conversation. He hadn't heard her voice in almost five years. "It's Knox."

There was a long pause on the other end.

"I'm sorry for calling you in the middle of the night," he said as he forced his legs to move him toward the window at the end of the hall. "I would have waited until morning, but—"

"I'm in Honolulu," she said. "It's only eleven here. I was just getting ready for bed." There was a muffled sound, and then he heard Reina say to someone else who was with her, "It's my ex-husband. He sounds desperate."

"I'm calling about Blair," Knox said. And he *was* desperate. He wanted Reina to care, for Blair and Addison's sake. He vividly recalled Blair's prayer that they could meet their mom.

Again, there was that pause, but then she said, "Is something wrong with her?"

"She's in emergency surgery. They are removing her appendix. I thought you might like to know."

It took a moment for Reina to respond, and when she did, her voice was flat. "Why does this matter to me, Knox? The girls are your responsibility. Are you hoping I'll fly into Minnesota and take care of her? If you do, you're out of your mind. I have far more important things to do with my time."

Knox's heart dropped at her cold response. What was more important than her daughters? "I don't want anything from you, Reina. I just thought, as her mother—"

"I am *not* that child's mother. If you don't need anything from me, there's no point continuing this conversation."

He didn't need anything, but he had wanted some kind of empathy or concern on her part. "You might not be her mother anymore, but I thought you might want to know."

"I don't. As far as I'm concerned, those girls are strangers to me. I have no wish to talk about them, worry about them or even think about them. They mean nothing to me."

"I'm sorry you feel that way."

"Where did you get this number? I purposely changed numbers after I left Minnesota so you couldn't contact me. I was afraid something like this would happen and you'd try to saddle me with those children."

Those children.

Her words felt like a deep stab at his heart. *Those* children meant everything to him. They were his very life.

"Well?" she asked.

He didn't want to get Merritt in trouble—didn't even

want to bring her into the conversation. It would cause nothing but pain for her.

"It doesn't matter, Reina. I'll be deleting your number as soon as we hang up, and you will never hear from me again."

"Good." The line went dead.

Knox pulled the phone away from his ear and stared at it before deleting her number. Anger and resentment knotted inside his chest. Blair was lying on an operating table in a cold room somewhere in this hospital and Reina didn't have the decency to care? What kind of a person could be so callous and unfeeling? Was it her way of coping? Or did she truly not think twice about the two little girls she had brought into this world?

He shoved his phone into his pocket and leaned his hands against the windowsill, dropping his head as he took several deep breaths. He blamed himself for all this. If he had been smarter or stronger or a better judge of character, then Reina would have never found a way into his life.

Yet, if she hadn't, he wouldn't have the girls —and he couldn't imagine a world in which they didn't live. He loved and adored them, and despite all the pain, he would do it all over again for them in a heartbeat.

A hand touched his shoulder, and he looked up to find Merritt there. Her brown eyes were filled with compassion and empathy, and it was all he needed.

He pulled her into his arms and held her tight.

She returned the hug, pressing her cheek against his chest. She fit snug against him, conforming to his body perfectly. Everything about her was warm and gentle, and he closed his eyes, drawing strength from her very presence. It seemed impossible that Merritt and Reina were sisters. They were as different as two people could be.

"I'm sorry," she whispered.

"Did you hear?"

"I heard what you said, and I can only imagine what she said."

He didn't want to let her go. She was everything Reina was not—everything he longed for and desired in a life partner. Everything he had hoped Reina would turn out to be.

Knox loved having her by his side, no matter if they were working, playing, laughing or crying. She eased the burdens, softened the rough patches and made everything better, whether good or bad.

And in that moment, he realized he wasn't just falling for her—he was falling in love with her.

"What am I going to do without you?" he whispered against her hair as he laid his lips upon her head. His feelings for her were so powerful, he was afraid if he said too much, he'd scare her off. He needed time to sort out what it all meant.

She didn't speak for a moment, yet he wanted to know her thoughts and feelings. He pulled back, hoping to look into her eyes, but when he did, he regretted it.

Tears rimmed her eyes—tears that he was afraid he had caused. One of them slipped past her eyelid and trailed down her cheek. He wasn't prepared to see her cry. It tore his heart in two, and he had the urge to do whatever it would take to make her smile again.

He lifted his finger and gently wiped away the tear. "Don't cry," he whispered. "It breaks my heart to see your tears."

She blinked several times and swallowed. "I'm

sorry—I just hate how she continues to hurt you and the girls. If I could take away the pain, I would."

So she wasn't crying because of Knox. She was crying because of Reina. "She has hurt you, too."

"It doesn't matter. I've been dealing with it all of my life. But you and the girls shouldn't have to."

"She won't be hurting them anymore," he said, feeling resolved to push Reina out of his life once and for all. "I won't let her continue to have anything to do with my pain or regret. It's time I move on and stop running from the past. I won't let anger or bitterness have a place in my life anymore. The girls deserve better—and to be honest, I do, too."

It was time he reassessed every aspect of his life, starting with his work schedule—and ending with his feelings for Merritt.

A hint of a smile lifted Merritt's lips—and Knox realized he was still holding her. The desire to kiss her was so overwhelming, he tightened his hold.

Her smile fell, and her gaze grew very serious. She stared up at him with both longing and trepidation, but she did not pull away.

Knox trembled with her nearness and with the overwhelming emotions he was feeling.

"Mr. Taylor?" A male voice broke into Knox's thoughts, pulling him from the path he'd been heading down.

Knox let Merritt go and turned to find Dr. Epley standing a few feet away. "How is Blair?"

"She's doing well and resting comfortably. The surgery went just as we expected, and thankfully we got in there before the appendix ruptured. She should be well enough to go home in two or three days."

"Thank you," Knox said, relief washing over him, making his legs feel weak.

"I'm happy to help," Dr. Epley said. "We'll monitor her through the night, and one of you is more than welcome to stay with her. She should be up and about in the morning, but we will hold off on feeding her until tomorrow evening."

"Can we see her now?" Merritt asked.

"She'll be in recovery for about an hour, but as soon as we have her settled in her room, you may go in and see her. A nurse will come and find you when she's ready."

"Thank you," Merritt said as she wiped at more tears.

"I hope you folks have a good night," he said, but then he glanced at his watch. "Or, should I say, morning?"

Knox smiled at the doctor as he turned and left them, then he looked to Merritt. "I'm so thankful she'll be all right."

Merritt smiled and nodded. "So am I."

"Would you mind if I stayed here with her tonight? After we see her, Addy should get home and try to get more sleep."

"No, I don't mind at all."

"Good." Knox couldn't imagine leaving Blair now.

Merritt continued to look up at him, expectation and questions in her eyes, but Knox was thankful for the doctor's interference. He wasn't prepared to share what was on his heart with Merritt—not only because of his own uncertainties about the future, but because of hers.

Chapter Twelve

It had been three days since they had rushed Blair to the emergency room, but Merritt felt as if an eternity had passed. Knox had spent every moment at the hospital, while Merritt had taken care of the house, the dog and Addy. The hardest part had been keeping Addy entertained and patient while she counted down the hours to Blair's release. They had come to visit several times, but it wasn't enough for either girl, who had never spent a night apart from each other until now.

"Are we almost there?" Addy asked for the tenth time since leaving Tucker Lake twenty minutes ago.

"Yes," Merritt said, forcing herself to be patient with her niece. "Do you see the hospital?" She pointed out the front of the car.

"And Blair can come home today?" Addy asked once again from the back seat.

"Yes. She should be just about ready when we get up to her room."

"Can we go swimming when we get home? Can we play with Ronnie? Can we go to the park or to the zoo?"

"Sweetie, I already told you that Blair will need to

take it easy for a couple of weeks until she's feeling better. She isn't even supposed to walk up the stairs for a while. She won't be able to play outside or swim today. She needs to do quiet activities like read books, color, play with Play-Doh or watch movies."

Addy frowned and crossed her arms, her bottom lip protruding.

The hospital was busy as Merritt parked the car and then waited for Addy to get out of her booster seat. The little girl practically ran toward the main entrance, her blond pigtails bouncing on either side of her head.

"Wait for me," Merritt cautioned her.

"I can't wait to tell Blair-bear about *all* the surprises we have at home." Addy clapped her hands together as she waited for Merritt inside the hospital's lobby.

"You can't tell her or they won't be a surprise."

Addy giggled and put her hand up to her mouth as she squealed in delight.

Her excitement was infectious, and Merritt smiled as she took Addy's hand and walked her to the bank of elevators on the far wall.

The smell of disinfectant wash filled Merritt's nose as they entered the elevators.

"Do you think she'll like our surprises?" Addy asked, looking up at Merritt with her bright blue eyes.

"I think she'll love them."

One of the ways Merritt had preoccupied Addy was preparing the house for Blair's return. They had gone shopping and found lots of fun indoor activities for Blair to do during her recovery. There were also balloons and flowers and a Welcome Home sign waiting for her return. Some of her favorite foods were in the kitchen, and they had brought a few of her toys down from her bedroom to keep her company on the couch in the great room.

Merritt and Addy had come to visit often enough that Addy knew exactly which button to press. Soon they were on the pediatrics floor, walking toward Blair's room.

Anticipation bubbled up in Merritt's stomach as she thought about taking Blair and Knox home with them. The house had been so quiet these past three days. And though they'd seen each other a bit, it hadn't been enough. She'd only had a short amount of time with Knox and Blair since coming back from South Carolina, and she didn't want to waste another second.

Addy let go of Merritt's hand and ran ahead to Blair's hospital room. She pushed open the door and said, "Blair! We're here!"

Merritt followed her into the room and was met with wide grins from both Blair and Knox. All around the bed, on the windowsill and at the counter were flowers, balloons and cards from friends and family. Even Merritt's parents had ordered flowers to be sent when Merritt had called them to share the news about Blair's surgery. Their vacation was almost over, but they hoped to get to Timber Falls sometime that autumn to see the girls. Along with the flowers, they had sent two teddy bears, one for each of the girls.

"I hope you brought a moving van to haul all of this stuff home," Knox teased Addy as she jumped into his arms. "I don't know where we're going to put all of it."

Addy giggled and then wiggled out of his arms to get on the bed with Blair, who was dressed in the outfit Merritt had brought from home yesterday.

Knox glanced up at Merritt, and she returned his

smile, happy that they were soon going to be free of the hospital.

But what would happen when they didn't have the distraction of the hospital to prevent them from discussing what had almost happened the other night before Dr. Epley interrupted them? Merritt had thought about it several times since then, but each time she had tried to push it away. Her interview with Timber Falls Community Christian School was tomorrow, and she had not yet heard from Oakhill Academy. What would happen if she was offered the job in Timber Falls? Would it be smart to accept the position with this strange new connection she had made with Knox? And what was the connection, exactly?

The questions went around and around in her head, yet she had no answers.

For the next half an hour, Merritt stayed with the girls while Knox loaded all the gifts into the back of his SUV. Blair was in great spirits, happy to be going home, and her incision had been healing nicely, so she was in very little pain.

The girls talked incessantly as Merritt packed each vase of flowers into the boxes the nurses provided. And when everything was ready to go and they had been given the discharge papers, they walked alongside Blair, who was wheeled out of the hospital by a nurse.

Several people waved to her as she went, and the grin on her face told Merritt the little girl felt like a rock star right about now.

Finally, the four of them were in the SUV, pulling out of the parking lot, on their way home.

"This is a much more pleasant car ride than the last

one the four of us took together," Knox said to Merritt as he drove the SUV toward home.

"All's well that ends well." Merritt quoted something her mother had often said to her growing up. "I'm so thankful for modern medicine and God's gift of healing."

They were quiet for a moment as they drove through downtown Timber Falls and headed north out of town.

Merritt glanced at Knox, and he turned to smile in her direction. "Thank you for all your help these past few weeks," he said. "But especially the past few days. It was comforting to know that you were taking care of Addy and Darby for me."

"You're welcome. I'm so happy I could be here." It was a privilege to be a part of their life, one she would never take for granted.

"Your interview with the Christian school is tomorrow," Knox said. "Are you ready?"

"I think so." Nervous excitement rushed up her spine at the thought. She had never loved interviews, but this one was especially intimidating. She wanted to love the school and dislike it, all at the same time. If she didn't like the school or the principal, it would be easier to turn down. If she loved it, then it would make her want to stay in Timber Falls all the more. She'd never felt so torn before in her life.

"I don't know much about the school," Knox said as he turned onto a county road, "other than the fact that it's really new. This will only be the second school year, but I've heard really good things about it. Blair and Addison are enrolled in the kindergarten class this fall."

Merritt looked at Knox, her mouth slipping open. "I

hadn't even considered where they'd be going to school this fall. If I should happen to get the job—"

"You might be their teacher."

A smile lifted Merritt's lips as she thought about what it would be like to have Blair and Addy in her class every day. It was a far more appealing prospect than only seeing them a couple times a year.

"Are you going to be our teacher, Auntie Merritt?" Blair asked from the back seat.

"I don't know, sweetheart," she admitted. "I have a lot of tough decisions to make—but it all depends on if they offer me the job."

"I hope you're our teacher," Addy said. "You'd be the best teacher ever."

Their precious voices warmed Merritt's heart. Of all the kindergarten students she'd ever had, they would be her favorite, by far.

Twenty minutes later, they were pulling into Knox's garage. He turned off the engine, and Merritt got out to help Blair with her seat belt while Knox assisted Addy.

"We have a surprise for you!" Addy told her sister. "Come in and see."

Blair slowly got out of the car and walked gingerly toward the service door with Merritt and Knox right behind.

The smell of food met Merritt's nose the moment they entered the house. It almost smelled like garlic and marinara.

"Did you leave something in the Crock-Pot for supper?" Knox asked Merritt as he set Blair's bag in the entryway.

Merritt shook her head. "No. I was planning on

making baked macaroni and cheese for supper, since it's Blair's favorite."

"Yoo-hoo!" came a voice from the back of the house. "Is that you, Knox?"

"Penelope," Merritt said under her breath.

It was going to be a long night.

"What is going on here?" Knox asked as he brought his family into the kitchen.

Penelope was sitting at the kitchen island, a drink in hand, while her cook stood at the stove managing several boiling pots of noodles, sauce and green beans.

"It is you," Penelope said as she stood and smoothed back her hair. She approached Knox and put her hand on his arm, her shoulders coming up in glee. "Surprise. I hope you don't mind that I showed myself in to make you a nice little family-style supper tonight for Blair's welcome home."

Knox frowned as he looked around the kitchen, wondering what part of the meal Penelope was making. "That wasn't necessary, Pene—"

"Nonsense." She squeezed his arm. "You've all been through so much these past few days, I wanted to do something nice for you." She turned to Blair and bent at the waist to address her. "And look at you, darling. All pale and skinny. You need to get right to bed, young lady. Do you hear me? I'm sure your nanny will see to your needs while your daddy and I relax a little bit on the back patio." She stood straight again, and her voice lowered. "He deserves some rest, and I know just what he needs."

Merritt, Blair and Addy all looked at Knox with wide eyes. If they were anything like him, they had been looking forward to a little peace and quiet this evening. Some normalcy. They'd had enough of nurses and doctors barging in on them at all hours of the day. Having Penelope in his home—uninvited—was a recipe for disaster and a bad precedent to set. He needed to get rid of her, and he was afraid that if he wasn't straightforward, she wouldn't get the hint.

"We're all tired," Knox said to Penelope. "Maybe it wasn't such a good idea to come over tonight."

"You're just saying that to be polite." Penelope turned so she was facing Knox, her back to Merritt and the girls. "You don't need to play coy with me, Knox Taylor. We can be honest with each other. I know your manners dictate that you tell me these things, but in your heart, I know you're happy to see me. It's been four long days since you and the girls came over for supper. I miss you."

Knox hadn't mentioned to Merritt that Penelope had practically dragged him into her house to eat supper the night before she came back from South Carolina. The girls had been playing with Veronica that day while he had worked, and when he went to retrieve them, she refused to let him leave without eating first.

But he knew how much Merritt didn't like Penelope, so he hadn't said anything.

Enough was enough. "Penelope, I know your intentions are good." *Maybe.* "But we really just want a quiet evening together. Merritt, Blair, Addy and myself."

Penelope lifted her chin as her eyebrow came up. "Oh. I see."

"I appreciate the food you brought over—but I understand if you want to take it back home with you," Knox continued. "Merritt had other plans for supper tonight."

The cook stopped stirring the sauce and looked between Penelope and Knox.

Penelope cast her cool gaze on Merritt for the first time since they had entered the room and offered her an aloof glance. "I see perfectly."

Merritt lifted her chin, just a bit, as she put her hands around the girls' shoulders.

"Well," Penelope said. "If I'm not wanted, I know how to take the hint."

"I don't mean to offend," Knox said quickly. "We just need a bit of time to recover from the last few days. We'll be happy to see you and Veronica when Blair is feeling up to company. Call or text me in a few days and I'll let you know."

"That's fine, that's fine," Penelope said, raising her hand to stop him from talking. "Come along, Sandy," she said to the cook. "We're being an inconvenience to the Taylors."

Sandy looked at the food on the stove and took a tentative step away.

"Just leave it," Penelope said to her in a harsher tone. "Though I doubt *Merritt* has the ability to step in and take over what someone else has started."

Knox frowned and met Merritt's gaze. Penelope's comment seemed to hit a soft spot in her, and she looked down at the ground.

"Good night," Knox said as he went to the door and opened it for Penelope and Sandy to leave. "Thank you for your thoughtfulness."

Penelope just rolled her eyes as she and Sandy left the house.

Darby stood up from her dog bed and wagged her tail as she came to the door. Knox opened it again to let her out, and when he closed it behind her, he turned to his girls.

All three of them.

"Well," he said with a forced smile. "It's not baked macaroni and cheese, but it looks like it's almost finished. Who's hungry?"

"I'm tired," Blair said as she slumped against Merritt's side.

"Oh, sweetie." Merritt gently lifted the girl into her arms. "I'm sorry. Addy and I have a special surprise waiting for you in the great room."

Knox turned off the burners on the stove and followed Merritt and the girls into the next room.

They had brought Blair's quilt down from her bed and put it on one of the sofas with several of her favorite stuffed animals. A large banner hung on the upper balcony railing and said, Welcome Home, Blair! And there were balloon bouquets everywhere.

Blair's face lit up as she took it all in.

"And we got your favorite ice cream and Auntie Merritt is going to make all your favorite foods," Addy said to her. "And look." She went to the coffee table in front of the sofa and jumped up and down as she pointed to the new coloring books, crayons, stickers and games stacked there. "We're going to have lots of fun, Blairy, even if we can't go swimming."

Knox loved that Addy had taken on Blair's limitations so that Blair wouldn't be the only one who couldn't go outside.

Merritt set Blair down on the sofa and laid her blanket over her before sitting down next to her. "What do you think?"

Blair smiled. "I love it. Thank you."

"You're welcome." Merritt allowed Addy to climb into her lap. "Addy picked out most of the crafts and games."

"Because I know just what you like," Addy said with a toothless grin.

Knox leaned up against the archway, his heart warming with affection for Merritt and the girls. Never in his life had he felt so complete or whole. Never had he felt so peaceful or content. This, right here, was exactly what he had always wanted. Suddenly, he felt no need to leave Tucker Lake ever again. No longing to see far-off places or exotic locales. Anything and everything his heart desired was right here in his very own home.

"How about I go finish supper?" Knox said to the girls. "I'm starving, and it smells really good."

"I'll help," Merritt said as she left Blair and Addy to look at all the fun new activities.

Knox welcomed her help with a smile, and they re-entered the kitchen.

"I hated kicking Penelope out like that," he said to her. "It's such an awkward position to be in."

Merritt went to the refrigerator, where she pulled out a bag of lettuce. "Did you want her to stay?"

"No," Knox was quick to answer. "But it's still awkward. I know that she means well, she just doesn't always know how to handle the situation."

He went to the stove and checked the noodles, which looked about done. The sauce was also steaming and looked ready to eat. That's when he noticed the oven was on, and he checked inside to find some garlic bread, perfectly browned.

Merritt was quiet as she made the salad and got out the dishes to set the table.

Knox didn't like to see her so reserved, so he asked her, "Something on your mind?"

She looked up at him, her expression hard to read. "A lot of things."

But it was the only answer she gave him.

He had a lot of things on his mind, too. Things he wasn't ready to discuss, either.

Chapter Thirteen

The next morning, Merritt borrowed Knox's SUV and returned to Timber Falls to meet with the principal of the Christian school. As she pulled into the parking lot, she took a deep breath, praying for peace and clarity. She had been asking God what He wanted her to do about her job situation but hadn't felt peace either way. Instead, she chose to walk in faith, believing that He would give her the answer at the right time. Nothing had gone as planned this past summer, reminding her that her best-laid plans were not always God's.

Timber Falls Community Christian School had been added on at the back of the church, so Merritt was a little bit familiar with the layout. She hadn't gone into the school but had admired the new building from the parking lot outside. It was nestled in the midst of an older neighborhood with beautiful Victorian homes all around. A playground and the public library were close at hand, and the trees lining the street were mature, offering beautiful shade on this sultry July day.

Merritt parked her car and went to the main entrance of the school. The doors were locked, so she pressed the doorbell, which had a camera above it. She smiled, hoping to make a good first impression.

"Miss Lane?" said a voice over the intercom.

"Yes," Merritt said.

"Come on in."

The door unlocked, and Merritt pulled it open. Air-conditioning bathed her hot skin as she entered the hallway.

Everything looked new and pristine, and it smelled like fresh lemon polish. A display case in the front boasted two shiny trophies, one for speech and one for golf, while a large, framed picture showed all the smiling students from the previous year. It was an impressive number of children, given the newness of the school.

"Miss Lane?" a woman asked as she came out of a room with a sign overhead that said Office.

Merritt smiled and reached out to shake her hand. "Miss Sutton?"

"Yes, I'm Willa Sutton. It's so nice to meet you. Won't you come into my office?"

Willa Sutton was much younger than Merritt had anticipated. She was tall and graceful, with light brown hair twisted into a bun at the back of her head. She wore a long black pencil skirt and a white button-down shirt with a pair of black heels. Her style was simple yet graceful.

"The school is beautiful," Merritt said. "I've heard that it was built last year."

"It was. We're still learning the ins and outs of the building and establishing our reputation in Timber Falls. It's been a challenge, but I love challenges."

An older woman sat behind the front desk, and she smiled at Merritt.

"This is Mrs. Cortez," Willa said. "She's my administrative assistant and the backbone to this school."

Mrs. Cortez stood to shake Merritt's hand. She had a kind face and a welcoming smile, and Merritt liked her immediately. "I'm also the grandma to one of the incoming kindergartners," she said. "Sadie can't wait to start school. It's all she can talk about. But her mama and I aren't quite so excited. It's hard to send that first one off to school, isn't it?"

"I know exactly what you mean," Merritt said. "It goes by fast, doesn't it?" She was thinking about Blair and Addison and how quickly they had grown between visits.

"My office is this way," Willa said to Merritt.

"It was nice to meet you." Merritt waved to Mrs. Cortez.

"I sure hope we get to see you around here more often," Mrs. Cortez said with a wink and a smile.

Willa held the door open for Merritt and indicated one of the chairs across from her desk. "Won't you have a seat? Could I get you something to drink? Coffee? Water?"

"No, thank you." Merritt's hands were already shaking more than necessary. She couldn't imagine adding caffeine to her system.

After Willa took her seat, she offered Merritt a wide smile. "I have a confession to make. This is the first interview I've ever conducted. I was just hired as the principal earlier this summer. Before I came to Timber Falls, I was a high school English teacher in Virginia. So, if you're nervous, Miss Lane, please don't be. We're both in this together."

Merritt felt her stress melt away at Willa's honesty and warmth. "Please, call me Merritt."

"And you must call me Willa." She pulled out a file with Merritt's résumé and looked it over while she asked Merritt several questions about her education, her previous employment and her favorite aspects of being a teacher.

In return, Merritt asked Willa about the school, the staff and the families that attended. Willa had limited experience, but she told her everything she had learned since coming in early June. Merritt asked her why the previous principal and kindergarten teacher left, and Willa explained that the principal had been filling in for the interim. He had been a retired principal who attended the church but had only planned to get the school up and running before hiring Willa. And the kindergarten teacher had gotten married and moved out of state.

"From what I've heard," Willa said, "neither one wanted to leave, but circumstances dictated it."

When the interview came to an end, Willa asked Merritt if she'd like to see the classroom.

"I'd love to." Everything Merritt had learned about the school and the principal was wonderful. The more she spoke with Willa, the more excited she became.

The contrast between Timber Falls Community Christian School and Oakhill Academy was significant. Oakhill was established, rooted and offered an excellent legacy, whereas Timber Falls was new, hopeful and laying the groundwork for the hundreds of students and teachers that would come after. While

Merritt loved the idea of joining a long-standing team, she was equally excited about the possibility of establishing a foundation for a new school.

Merritt followed Willa out of the office and down the hallway. The very first room on the right was the K1 classroom. Willa turned on the light, and Merritt's heart warmed at the colorful room. Low tables and chairs sat in the middle with an art center in one corner, a book center in the other and the teacher's desk in the third. Big windows faced the back of the public library, with a glimpse of the playground. It was a bright, airy space, and Merritt could immediately imagine how she'd decorate. She could almost see the little boys and girls coming in, hanging their coats and backpacks on the hooks along the wall, snuggling up together in the reading corner to discover a new book, and getting messy in the art center, creating masterpieces to share with their parents and grandparents.

"We don't have a library in the school," Willa said. "Instead, we utilize the public library right next door. I've heard it worked very well for us last year, and the staff at the library loves our students."

"How nice."

"We also utilize parent and grandparent volunteers extensively," she continued. "They come in to help in the classrooms, on the playground and in the lunchroom. I've been told that no matter what you need, the families are very active and love to help out."

"I like the sound of that." Merritt smiled. She had met several of the families who sent their kids to this school, like the Ashers and the Harrises. Knowing she would have such great support was appealing.

Willa walked to the door. "I am planning to interview two more candidates early next week. I hope to make a final decision soon after."

"That sounds great." Merritt had not yet heard back from Oakhill, and the longer it took, the more she doubted that she would be selected. What if Timber Falls was her only option? What if she wasn't offered this job, either? What would she do with herself this year?

The ladies left the kindergarten room, and Willa gave Merritt a quick tour of the rest of the school. All too soon, it was time to leave.

"Thank you for coming," Willa said to Merritt. "You helped to make my first interview painless. I appreciate that very much."

"Thank you for asking me to come. I loved getting to know you and familiarizing myself with the school. My nieces will be enrolled here this fall."

"Oh, really?" Willa stopped and offered Merritt a curious smile. "What are their names?"

"Blair and Addison Taylor."

"Yes! I've seen their names on the roster. How exciting. We love when families are able to learn together. I'll definitely keep that in mind as I consider this position."

Merritt said goodbye and went back to the parking lot. Knox's SUV was hot as she climbed inside, but she didn't mind. She had so many things to consider, and coming to the school only made her decision that much harder. She loved the school, the classroom and the principal.

If she was offered both jobs, how would she ever decide?

* * *

Knox stood up and stretched. He'd been sitting at his computer in a Zoom meeting with his boss for the past hour and was ready for a break. When he'd left the girls in the great room, he had told them they could interrupt him only in an emergency, but they needed to keep quiet and busy on their own. The last time he'd seen them, they were playing with Play-Doh at the coffee table.

He stepped out of his office and checked his phone to see if he'd missed a call or text from Merritt. She had left that morning for her interview and hadn't come home yet. He didn't know how long the interview was supposed to last, but it had been four hours. He had thought she'd be back by now.

"Are you done, Daddy?" Addison asked when he entered the great room. The girls had turned on the television and were watching one of their favorite cartoons. Blair was lying on the couch, snuggled up in her pajamas with her blanket and stuffed animals close by. Addy was sitting in a recliner, her hands behind her head.

"I am," Knox said. "Thank you for being so quiet while I had my meeting."

"I made you lunch!" Addy jumped off the recliner and ran toward the kitchen. "Wanna see it?"

Blair didn't get up but stayed on the couch. She had been tired most of the day, and he had told her that whenever she needed a rest, she should listen to her body. So, instead of jumping up to follow Addy and Knox into the kitchen, she stayed on the couch and kept watching the show.

"You shouldn't be working in the kitchen by yourself, Addison." Knox cringed to think about what kind of a mess she had made. "I hope you didn't use the stove or any sharp knives. You know better, right?"

"Of course, Daddy," she said with an exasperated tone. "Mrs. Masterson said I can't use grown-up things."

"Good."

"When can I?"

"What?"

"Use grown-up things?"

"Not until you're at least twelve—maybe older." Knox had no idea when a child was capable of using a knife, so he gave her his best guess. It was moments like this that he wished he had someone more experienced at hand to answer his daughter's questions.

They entered the kitchen, and Addy ran to the refrigerator. She pulled out a tray with a bowl of cereal drenched in milk, a small apple, which rolled around the platter, and a long carrot that hadn't been peeled.

"Wow, Addy." Knox nodded, not sure how to describe what he thought. "That looks like—like a great lunch. Thank you."

She grinned from ear to ear.

He took the tray from her and set it on the counter.

"Aren't you going to eat it?" She looked up at him with her big blue eyes.

"Um." He wasn't a fan of cereal to begin with, but mushy cereal was even worse. Yet, how could he not eat what she had made for him? Slowly, he lifted the spoon out of the bowl. The cereal was swollen and soggy, but he was being watched closely by his daughter and didn't want to disappoint her. He lifted the cereal to his lips and took a bite.

"Mmm." He smiled as he forced himself to swallow the mush. "This is wonderful."

It wasn't true in the sense that the food was good, but in the heart behind her gift.

"Did you and Blair have lunch?" he asked.

"Not yet."

"How about I make that baked macaroni and cheese Merritt was going to cook last night and throw some chicken nuggets into the oven?"

"Okay."

"Would you like to help me?"

"Sure!"

As Addy helped Knox with lunch, the meal she had made him went unnoticed. Knox did pick up the apple and snacked on it while they waited for the macaroni and cheese to bake, which made Addy happy. And he got out a few more carrots to add to the one she had given him. They peeled them and cut them up to dip into ranch dressing.

The kitchen was beginning to smell delicious when the garage door finally opened. Addy was in the great room with Blair, who had fallen asleep on the couch. Darby was on the floor in front of the couch, which was where she'd been staying since Blair had come home from the hospital, and Knox was in the kitchen, waiting for the timer to go off.

He didn't leave the kitchen, though he had the urge to meet Merritt in the entryway to hear about her day. The last thing he needed her to know was that he'd been counting down the minutes for her to return. He wanted to know how the interview had gone, and more than anything, he hoped and prayed that she loved the school in Timber Falls and wanted to stay. It would

allow them more time and space to explore their growing relationship.

Yet—he suddenly wondered if Merritt longed for
the same thing. Did her feelings run as deep as his?
Would she even consider pursuing a relationship with
him? Or did she still think of him as one of those types
of men she had spent her life avoiding?

He was at the counter, looking at his emails, when
he heard Merritt talking to Addy. His pulse ticked a
little higher when Merritt said she was going to check
on lunch.

"Hello," she said when she entered the kitchen. "It
smells great in here."

"Baked macaroni and cheese. I hope you don't mind
that I made it without you."

She shook her head and went to the coffeepot to
pour herself a cup. "I'm starving."

Knox set down his phone and asked the question
he'd been wondering for hours. "How did the interview go?"

Merritt took a moment to finish making her coffee,
and when she finally turned around to look at him, he
had a hard time reading her expression. She looked
torn. "The school is amazing, and the principal is great.
I only met one other staff member, but she was also
very sweet. From everything Willa told me, it sounds
like a wonderful place to work."

Hope surged in Knox's chest. Did that mean she was
going to stay? "That sounds awesome, Merritt. Did she
offer you the job?"

"No." She let out a sigh and then took a sip of her
coffee. "She has a couple other candidates to interview
before she makes her final decision."

Disappointment dipped inside Knox, and he found himself nodding, trying hard not to let his emotions show. "Do you know when that might be?"

"By the end of next week at the latest."

"And still nothing from Oakhill?"

Merritt shook her head. "I don't know why it's taking them so long to decide. Unless they already did and they're just taking their time letting me know that someone else got it."

"I don't think that's it." He smiled, hoping to cheer her. "How will you choose between Oakhill and Timber Falls Community Christian School? Because I have a feeling you're going to get offers from both."

Merritt quirked her mouth. "That would definitely be the best-case scenario. I really don't think that'll be the case. I might not get either one."

The timer went off. Knox stood and grabbed the oven mitts to remove the macaroni and cheese. Merritt was standing close to the oven, so she moved aside, but she was still close enough that Knox could smell her perfume. It was subtle and sweet. And she looked amazing in a pair of black capri pants, a white T-shirt and a black blazer, rolled at the sleeves.

"You look great, by the way," he said to her.

She glanced at him, a gentle smile on her lips. "Thanks."

After he pulled out the macaroni and cheese and the chicken nuggets, he set them on cooling racks.

"Blair was asleep and Addy looked like she was about to take a nap," Merritt said to Knox. "Do you think we should wait for them to wake up before we eat?"

Knox walked to the doorway and peeked into the great room. Both girls were fast sleep.

He rejoined Merritt in the kitchen again. "They've had a big week. I'd hate to wake them up now." He paused as he glanced outside. "We can let this cool off for a little while as I show you something."

Merritt put down her coffee cup. "Sure."

Knox tilted his head toward the door. "Follow me."

The look of curiosity on Merritt's face warmed his heart. She was always up for an adventure, and he loved how easygoing she was, even when she had no idea what he had in mind.

"I hope you love it," he said.

"I'm sure I will." Her dimples appeared as she smiled, and Knox knew, in that moment, that he was going to have to work hard to convince her to stay in Timber Falls.

Because he didn't want to wake up every day for the rest of his life knowing he wasn't going to see that smile.

Chapter Fourteen

Merritt followed Knox out the back door, across the patio and toward the stand of white pine on the edge of his property. She'd almost forgotten about the playhouse.

"Are we going to the playhouse?"

"Did you check it out while I was at the hospital with Blair?" he asked as they walked across the side yard.

"No." She shook her head. "I was too distracted. I didn't even think about it."

He grinned. "It's finished."

"What?" She stopped and touched his arm. "Seriously?"

"We finished it while you were in South Carolina. I was going to show it to you the day after you came back, but then everything happened with Blair and it slipped my mind."

"I'm not surprised." She had been so impressed with his dedication to Blair. No wonder he'd forgotten all about the playhouse.

"It turned out amazing," he said, taking her hand. "I can't wait for you to see it."

She let him hold her hand as they walked, and though it should have felt awkward, it didn't. Merritt loved how strong and capable yet gentle and reassuring his hands were. His touch felt right—perfect—filling her with joy and comfort. But it was more than that. He also made her feel excited and full of anticipation, and not just for the playhouse, but for life in general. Brad had never made her feel those things. Her life with him had looked predictable and settled. With Knox, Merritt could easily imagine adventure, excitement and fun, all while feeling grounded and rooted.

They walked through the trees until they came to the playhouse. Knox still held her hand as he watched her reaction.

It was beautiful—and so much more than a playhouse. It truly looked like a guest cottage. Everything was finished, from the gray siding to the white trim around the windows and doors. Even the flagstone path had been laid to the front door, and flowers were planted in the window boxes.

"After it was done," Knox said, "I realized it reminds me a lot of the cabin we used to stay in at the resort when I was a kid. It hadn't even occurred to me how much as I designed it."

"Knox." Merritt just shook her head in astonishment. "I had no idea it was going to be so charming."

"Do you like it?"

"Do I like it?" She looked up at him, completely in awe of his talent. "I love it."

He smiled down at her, his face glowing from her praise.

"How did you possibly get it finished?" she asked.

"I had a lot of time on my hands while you were

gone." He winked at her. "And I was able to hire a few guys to help out. Once the outside was done by Matt's construction team, it didn't take the electrician long to run the wires. After that, we insulated it and hung Sheetrock. Then it was mudded and taped, and after that we painted. All that was left was the flooring and the trim." He shrugged. "I'm sure I'll add more when it becomes a real guesthouse, but for now, it will work for the girls."

"I'm speechless."

"Would you like to see inside?"

Merritt nodded and allowed him to lead her into the house. When they stepped inside, he finally let go of her hand—leaving her to miss his touch more than she should.

The playhouse was one simple room, with wood floors and an area rug. The ceiling was vaulted, and a fan was hanging down from the center. There was no furniture inside yet, but it would easily fit a full-size bedroom set one day. The windows looked out three sides, and the front door faced the sparkling lake.

"I wonder what Noah Asher would think of this place?" Merritt asked Knox.

"It would probably be too fancy for him." He grinned.

"I think he'd love the sentiment behind it."

"I hope so." Knox moved to one of the windows facing his large house and looked outside. "The girls will have it full of their toys in no time. I'm sure they'll spend hours out here, and one day, down the road, they'll probably fill it with their giggling friends during sleepovers."

"It's hard to even imagine such a thing." And would Merritt be there to see it?

He kept looking outside, his face turning pensive, and he didn't say anything for a moment.

Merritt walked across the room and joined him. "Is everything okay?"

Knox sighed and gave her a sad smile. "I'm just thinking about the future. I had a meeting with my boss today, and he said he'd like to send me to Spain earlier than I had anticipated. And it sounds like the trip will last longer than I had planned."

Not knowing what to say, Merritt kept quiet.

"Now that I've been back here," he continued, "spending time with the girls, I've realized how much I don't want to go back to my other life. It scares me to think I might not be here next time one of the girls needs me." He paused and then turned his full attention on her. "Do you ever get the sense that you're wasting time?"

"Being engaged to Brad for six years made me feel that way all the time." She tried not to sigh. Surprisingly, it didn't sting so much thinking about Brad anymore. "I wanted to move on with my life and start living—really living—but every time I tried to push him, he found a reason to postpone."

Knox nodded. "I used to think that my lifestyle was exciting—and it was—but now it seems so trivial compared to being here with the girls. They won't be in my home forever, and one day I'm afraid I'm going to look back and regret all the years I missed with them—even more than I do now. I have to change things."

"What do you plan to do?"

He ran his hand over the back of his neck. "I have a

promising member of my team that's ready to take on more responsibility. She's single and loves to travel. If I give her the go-ahead, I know she'd like the opportunity."

"Is that what you want?"

"It's a big decision, and once I make it, I can't go back. It would be a permanent change."

"Are you ready for a permanent change?" She watched him carefully. Was he ready to commit to making such a big move?

"I hate to admit it, but I'm not sure. I want to be with the girls more than anything, but handing over my job to someone else feels like I'm taking a step backward in my career."

"It's okay to be uncertain, Knox. I have no idea what I'll do if I'm offered the job in Timber Falls—or if I'm not offered a job anywhere. It's scary, but if I've learned anything from my failed engagement, it's that God knows what's best for me. He knows what's best for you, too, and I believe He'll make it clear to both of us when the time is right."

Knox smiled at Merritt, his blue eyes soft and full of something she couldn't identify—or maybe she didn't want to. He had been looking at her this way since the night in the hospital when Dr. Epley had interrupted them. There was something powerful and profound in his gaze—dare she think it was love?

And, if it was, what did that mean? Was she ready for him to love her? More importantly, was she ready to love him?

Knox took a step closer to Merritt. "God has already started to make something clear in my heart."

Merritt caught her breath as he reached out and put

his hand on her cheek. The sun was shining off the lake, making the reflection shimmer through the windows into the cottage.

She didn't move or speak. His hand felt so tender on her face. She wanted to lean into its warmth and softness but refrained, uncertain what he was about to say to her.

"When you first came here," he said, "I remember talking to you on the patio that second night. You asked me if I was done with romance, and I told you that I wasn't sure it was worth the risk. But then you said, what if I found the love of my life? And I asked if you thought it was possible to have that kind of a love story. And you told me that you had to believe it was."

Merritt swallowed as her chest rose and fell on the short breaths she was taking. "I remember."

"What if I told you that you've made a believer out of me, Merritt?" He studied her closely, so many questions in his beautiful eyes. He slowly lowered his hand. "What if I told you that I think I have found the love of my life, in the very last place I ever thought to look?"

The cottage felt smaller and much more intimate as Merritt gazed into his face, trying to understand what he was saying to her. "Me?"

He nodded as he swallowed and drew her into his arms. "I've never known anyone like you, Merritt. You're smart, beautiful, kind, compassionate, courageous and so much more. You make me feel at home in my very own house for the first time in a long, long time. You complete my life in ways I didn't realize I was lacking."

Her heart pounded hard as he spoke, filling her with

such intense hope and longing, she thought she might burst.

"And the most important thing?" he continued. "You love Blair and Addison like they were your very own daughters."

But they weren't her daughters. She stiffened under his gentle touch. They were Reina's daughters. Merritt felt like a cold bucket of water had been dumped on her head. First and foremost, this was Reina's home and Reina's husband and Reina's life.

Merritt shook her head as she backed out of Knox's arms, despising herself for the thoughts and emotions swimming through her heart and mind. She felt sick thinking about everything she was going to toss away, simply because her sister had arrived first. But the very thought of being second-best filled her with panic and loathing for herself.

"I'm sorry, Knox." The panic swelled and tightened her throat. "I—I can't."

She didn't offer an explanation or try to make him understand. All she could think about was getting out of the cottage as fast as possible. But where would she go? And how would she ever face Knox again after what she'd just done?

He had offered her his heart, and she had thrown it back at him.

With no plan, she blindly entered the house and rushed up the stairs to her bedroom. It was the only sanctuary she could think of where she'd have time to be alone with her thoughts and regrets.

Knox stood for a long time in the playhouse, staring at the door Merritt had just exited. Pain and disappointment sliced through him, but more than that was regret. He shouldn't have said anything to her unless he had been certain she returned his feelings. He hadn't planned on it, but the moment had felt right. Yet it had placed both her and him in an awkward position. How would he face her again? What could he possibly say to make her feel comfortable in his presence? He had told her he had found the love of his life, but he couldn't claim she was the love of his life if she didn't return those feelings, could he?

He felt like a fool and a cad and a lovesick schoolboy. And now he probably didn't even have her friendship.

A hollow void filled his gut as he left the playhouse and walked back to his home, kicking a clump of dirt on the way. Merritt wasn't outside, at least, not that he could see. Where had she gone? Was she planning to leave? What must she be thinking?

All these questions were circling inside his mind as he stepped into the kitchen. The baked macaroni and cheese was still sitting on the counter cooling, and the television was still on in the great room. He walked across the kitchen to check on the girls, hoping Merritt was there.

He was embarrassed, but he wanted to talk to her. To clear the air and to reassure her that he didn't expect her to feel the same way he did, and that he didn't want her leaving before it was necessary.

The girls were still sleeping, so he quietly turned off the television and petted Darby, who looked up at him with big brown eyes. She didn't look like she was going to leave Blair's side anytime soon.

Had Merritt gone to her bedroom? Would she be

upset if he knocked on her door? He wanted to have an open and honest conversation with her, because if he knew anything about relationships, it was the need for clarity and transparency. It would be hard to face her right now—possibly the hardest thing he'd ever had to do—but it would be worth it if he could salvage any sort of friendship going forward.

The only thing that really worried him was how he would hide the depth of his love for her. Even if she didn't return his affection, that didn't mean his feelings had changed. But he didn't want to continue to upset her—or to embarrass himself. One rejection for the day was more than enough.

He stopped at the bottom of the steps, his heart feeling heavy, as he held the banister for a moment to steady his pulse and his thoughts. He did love Merritt, very much, and the thought of her walking away, of not returning his feelings, broke his heart like nothing ever had. But it hurt even more to think she was suffering alone right now. He didn't know why she couldn't give him her heart, but he had always suspected that he wasn't worthy anyway.

Without allowing himself another moment to second-guess his decision, he took the stairs two at a time and was soon outside Merritt's bedroom door. The afternoon sun was shining bright from the great room windows below as he knocked on her door.

"Merritt, can we talk?" he asked.

There was a pause, and then he heard shuffling in the room. Slowly, Merritt opened her bedroom door. Her eyes were full of tears, making Knox's knees weak at the sight of them. This time he *knew* he had caused them, and he felt horrible.

"Mere, I'm so sorry."

She pushed a lock of hair behind her ear and shook her head. "It's okay, Knox. It's not your fault."

"What do you mean? I shouldn't have said what I said. Of course it's my fault." He wanted to reach out and pull her into his arms, but he knew it would be foolish. It was the last place she wanted to be right now. Hadn't she just proved that to him?

"I'm sorry, Knox." She wiped at her cheeks and lifted her chin. Her brown eyes were so full of pain and uncertainty. "I—I have come to care for you, very much. You are so dear to me. It's just—" She paused and swallowed as she looked down at her hands. "There are just some things that neither of us can change."

She didn't love him. He could see it all over her face and hear it in her voice. And he knew, instinctively, that it wasn't just about him and her—it was about Reina, too. His past with Reina was the thing they couldn't change. And even if they could, would she love him?

He took a step back, feeling cold at the thought of his past. He regretted his decisions more than anyone, and never more so than this moment. He shouldn't be surprised at her admission. She had made it clear that she had never been interested in Reina's type.

"If things were different," Merritt said, beseeching him with her eyes. "If we had met a different way—" She shook her head. "I just can't—" She paused again, her dimples prominent as she pressed her lips together.

There was no point in continuing this conversation. He couldn't change the past, couldn't change his mistakes. And he wasn't going to try to beg Merritt to love him anyway. He was the sum of his past experiences, good and bad, and if she couldn't see beyond those mistakes, then there was no hope for their relationship.

"You don't need to worry about me saying anything again," he said to her. "I don't want you to leave before the girls' party, so let's try to make things as normal as we can, okay?"

She nodded and swallowed, wiping at her cheeks again. "Okay."

He turned and left her room, struggling to put one foot in front of the other.

Knox had always known that his poor choices would follow him for the rest of his life. He had suffered the consequences in so many other ways, but he had never thought that it would come to this. That once he discovered a happily-ever-after *was* possible, his past would come back and laugh in his face. Would he ever be free of Reina's destruction?

The macaroni and cheese still smelled delicious, but he no longer had an appetite. He went into the kitchen and put a lid on the casserole dish and put it into the refrigerator for the girls when they woke up.

Hopefully by then, he and Merritt would be able to be in each other's company without it feeling awkward, but he doubted it, very much.

Chapter Fifteen

It had been a week since the conversation in the playhouse with Knox, and Merritt still relived every moment of it each time she closed her eyes. Despite promising him it would be normal again between them, it had been anything but. The week had been painful, to say the least, as they had tried to coexist in the same home without talking about what had passed between them. Every time they looked at each other, she knew what he was thinking, and it would cause her embarrassment and regret to surge again.

Knox had been a gentleman, but she knew he was hurt, and she hated that she had been the one to hurt him. He had grown distant, putting physical and emotional space between them, and she didn't blame him. She could hardly look herself in the mirror each morning and face the truth: she was a coward. Instead of confronting her irrational fears of being second-best, or giving up her pride, she was letting the very best man she'd ever known slip away from her. And she felt powerless to change. Every time she thought she might, the same panic overcame her.

It was Thursday afternoon, and Knox was in his office on a Zoom meeting while Merritt sat on the dock watching the girls swim. Blair was feeling like her old self again and had promised Merritt that she wouldn't play rough in the water. The girls were on their floaties, and Merritt let her feet dangle in the cool water, soaking up the heat of the late-July sunshine. Darby lay beside her, watching the girls carefully and lifting her head to look at the passing speedboats playing in the lake.

"Who's that?" Addy asked, pointing toward the house.

Merritt turned and shaded her eyes as she looked in the direction Addy was pointing. Her mouth dropped open as she scrambled to her feet. "It's my mom and dad."

"Who?" Addy asked.

"It's my mom and dad!" Merritt said, a little more excited. "Your grandma and grandpa Lane."

The girls stared at Merritt's parents, but Merritt couldn't stay where she was. She jogged across the lawn, grinning as she opened her arms wide and embraced first her mom and then her dad. "What are you two doing here?" She could hardly believe they had come.

"We left Ireland and returned to Charleston on Sunday," Mom said, "and I told George we couldn't waste another moment, so we purchased tickets to Minneapolis for today."

Merritt's heart warmed at their arrival, and she shook her head. "Why didn't you tell me?"

"We wanted it to be a surprise," Dad said.

"But we rented a hotel room in Timber Falls," Mom continued. "So we won't be an imposition."

"Knox has another guest room," Merritt said. "You don't need to stay at a hotel."

Mom and Dad looked at each other, and then Mom said, "Given all that's happened between our family and Knox, we didn't want to presume."

"But we're family," Merritt insisted. "I know he'll want you to stay." Knox was one of the most hospitable men she'd ever met. She couldn't imagine him turning her parents out. "And if you stay, you can enjoy the lake and the girls even more."

"Speaking of the girls," Mom said as she looked past Merritt's shoulder, "are you going to introduce us?"

Merritt turned and found the girls exactly where she had left them. "Yes! Come on. I'm sure you're anxious to get to know them."

Mom and Dad followed Merritt as she called, "Blair. Addison. Come and meet your grandparents."

The girls paddled their floaties to the shore and stepped out. They looked equally uncertain as they clasped hands and walked over to their grandparents. The girls were wearing matching pink swimming suits.

"This is Grandma and Grandpa Lane," Merritt said. "They're your mom's parents."

"Hello," Mom said to the girls. "It's so nice to see you. Do you know, the last time I held you in my arms, you weighed only five pounds each?" Mom showed them about how small that was with her hands. "And look at you now! All grown-up, and so beautiful. You look just like your mama when she was your age."

The girls looked at one another and then grinned and began to giggle.

Knox appeared at the kitchen door. He stepped onto

the patio and stood for a moment before he crossed the yard and joined them.

"Hello, George and Cathy," he said, reaching out and shaking first Dad's hand and then Mom's. "This is a nice surprise."

"We hope you don't mind," Mom said. "We just couldn't wait another minute to see these girls. And with Merritt here..." She let the sentence trail off.

"Of course I don't mind." Knox smiled and looked genuinely happy to see them. "I hope you'll be able to stay until the girls' party next weekend."

"That's exactly what we were hoping," Dad said. "We rented a room at a hotel in town for the next week."

Knox shook his head. "That's not necessary. I have plenty of room for you here. I would love for you to stay as long as you'd like."

Merritt smiled, thankful he was opening his home to her parents. They had always gotten along well, but after what had happened with Reina, she wasn't truly sure how he'd feel about them being at his house.

"That's so kind of you," Mom said to Knox. "Thank you. We'd love to stay."

"You're going to stay here?" Blair asked, her eyes big with excitement.

Mom nodded. "Would you like that?"

"Yay!" The girls both cheered.

"Did you know I had surgery?" Blair asked. "Right here on my tummy." She pointed to the spot.

Mom nodded, her face very sad. "I did. I hope you're feeling better."

"I'm all better!" Blair took Mom's hand and said, "Would you like to see our new playhouse?"

Addy followed Blair's lead and took Dad's hand

as the pair marched their grandparents off to find the playhouse.

Merritt smiled and shook her head in wonder. "I doubt we'll see them for the rest of the day. My mom and dad will be completely enthralled with those girls, and vice versa."

Knox nodded as he met Merritt's gaze. She could still see the hurt behind his eyes, and she hated that she had been the cause of it. "I'm happy they came," he said. "I hope that all of us can move past the heartache Reina caused and get on with our lives."

His words struck the tender spot in her heart she had been guarding this week, and all she could do was nod.

The day went by quickly as Merritt, Knox and the girls spent time with her parents. They laughed, played games and sat on the patio until the girls went to bed.

Later, as Knox was showing Dad his fishing supplies, Mom motioned for Merritt to follow her. "Help me get settled into our room," she said.

Merritt followed her mom into the house and up the stairs to the second guest room. Mom closed the door and nodded at the two chairs near the window.

Merritt's phone chimed, indicating she had an email. When she looked at it, she saw it was from Oakhill Academy. With shaking hands, she opened the email and read that they were offering her the teaching position.

"Is it good?" Mom asked.

"Very good. Oakhill wants me to work for them."

"Wow." But Mom didn't look as happy as Merritt would have suspected.

Merritt frowned. "Aren't you happy for me? Don't you want me in James Island, close to you and Dad?"

Mom sat on one of the chairs and pointed to the other. "You and I need to have a talk."

"I don't like the sound of that."

Mom was an older version of Merritt. They shared the same brown eyes and brown hair and the same dimples. Whenever Merritt saw her mom, she was reminded of what she would probably look like in the next twenty-five years. But they also had similar personalities, and her mother knew Merritt better than anyone else. When Mom said they needed to talk, Merritt prepared herself for some truths she usually wasn't ready to hear.

Merritt took a seat on the other chair and couldn't look her mom in the eyes. She suspected she knew what this was going to be about.

"I would have to be blind not to notice there's something between you and Knox." Mom leaned forward. "What happened?"

With a sigh, Merritt sank deeper into the chair. She shook her head. "He's in love with me."

Mom's eyes opened wide. "Did he tell you that?"

Knox hadn't really said he was in love with her, but he had said she was the love of his life. Wasn't that the same? She nodded.

"What did you tell him?" Mom asked.

Merritt shrugged. "I told him I couldn't do it."

"You couldn't do what?"

"Be second-best." Tears sprang to Merritt's eyes without warning. "Reina got to him first. All I'll ever be to him is his second choice."

Mom blinked several times as she frowned. "What are you talking about?"

"I've always been second-best to Reina—my whole

life." Merritt stood and hugged herself. "Ever since I can remember, she was the one who had all the boy-friends, had all the attention, had all the drama. Even when it came to you and Dad. Anytime something good would happen to me, Reina would swoop in and steal all the attention. The worst was when she would break someone's heart. Her dejected boyfriends often came to me, hoping I could pick up the pieces of their broken hearts. But they didn't want me—they still wanted her. Even if they tried to pursue me, I knew it was only to get to her."

"Merritt, you've never, ever been second-best to your dad and me." Mom also stood and joined Merritt. "The reason why Reina was always taking the attention off of you and putting it on herself is because she felt she could never measure up to you. Your grades were better, your behavior was better, your friends were nicer. She couldn't compete, so she tried to take the attention off of you and put it onto herself. Most often it was negative attention, but it didn't matter to Reina."

Merritt's frown didn't diminish—if anything, it grew deeper.

"But what does that have to do with Knox?" Mom asked.

"I told myself I would never date one of the boys she cast aside. I couldn't live with the knowledge that I wasn't his first choice. And Knox is more than just a guy she dated. Reina married him and had children with him."

"Does Knox still pine after Reina?"

Merritt shook her head, wiping at her tears.

"Does he still want to be married to her?"

"No."

"Then why would you think you're his second choice? Do you think that maybe Knox realizes he made a mistake with Reina and you're the *better* choice?"

Merritt hadn't thought of that.

"And," Mom continued, "think about this. Knox didn't come to you with a broken heart, looking for you to fix it, like all the others trying to get back to Reina. If anything, he was probably shocked to have you in his home, and you were the last person he was trying to connect with." She smiled, and her voice softened. "Just watching you two together, even with the obvious tension, told me a lot. You're a good team. A perfect fit." She chuckled. "I actually thought you two would be a better fit way back when Reina introduced us to him. I knew from the moment we spoke that although he was handsome and wealthy and all the things that usually attracted Reina, he wasn't her type. It didn't take Reina long to figure that out, too. He was simply in the wrong place at the wrong time. A casualty of Reina's unending war with herself and life."

Merritt thought through all the men Reina had dated and realized what Mom said was true. At his heart, Knox was nothing like the others. He was too kind and too good and too selfless. More importantly, not once since Merritt had been in his home had he shown any interest in restoring his relationship with Reina. The only time he'd asked about her was when he wanted to make Reina care about Blair and her surgery.

"Do you love him?" Mom asked quietly, putting her hands on Merritt's arms.

The truth had been there for a long time. She had simply been too scared to admit it to herself. "I do."

"Then don't make him suffer any longer than necessary. Don't make him pay for his mistakes for the rest of his life. Other than Blair and Addison, I don't think anything good has come from Knox's relationship with Reina. Perhaps you could change that."

Merritt's heart began to beat a new rhythm as she allowed herself to move past her preconceived ideas about being second-best. Maybe Mom was right. Maybe she wasn't the second choice, but the better choice. At least, the better choice for Knox.

Her heart felt light and joyful for the first time in weeks, and she smiled at her mom. "Thank you."

Mom gave her a hug. "I long to see you happy, Merritt. Truly happy. And I believe that Knox and those girls fill you with a joy you've never felt before. I can see it on your face, hear it in your voice and admire it in your eyes. You were all made for each other, and somehow, in God's infinite wisdom and knowledge, He had this all worked out."

"They do make me happy."

"Then don't waste another moment. Fight for what you want, regardless of anything that came before. Don't let Reina win again."

Merritt nodded.

Her phone rang, and she pulled out of Mom's embrace to look at the number. "It's the Timber Falls Christian school principal." Merritt had told her all about the two schools where she had interviewed.

Mom lifted her eyebrows. "Hopefully it's more good news."

"Hello?" Merritt asked after pressing the green button.

"Hi, Merritt. Sorry to call so late. This is Willa. Is now a good time to talk?"

Merritt moved away from her mom and went to the window. The sun was just about to set, causing a riot of colors to paint across the horizon. Knox was building a fire in the patio fire pit, talking with Dad.

"Now is great."

"I have wonderful news! I'd love to offer you the position as kindergarten teacher."

Merritt swallowed the rush of emotions at Willa's words.

Suddenly, everything had changed.

Knox squatted next to the fire pit as he spoke to George about the best fishing spots on Tucker Lake.

"I wouldn't call myself an avid fisherman," George said to Knox. "But I go as often as I have the opportunity."

"This is a great walleye lake." Knox put another log on the flames and then stood, wiping the bark chips off his hands. "In the morning, I'll take you to the best-kept secret on the lake. It's a little bay on the south side, tucked back behind some overhanging willow trees."

George's eyes grew big. "I can't wait."

"The best time to catch walleye is at sunrise or sunset, so we'll need to be ready to go about five thirty."

"I'll be on the dock at quarter after five."

Cathy poked her head out the kitchen door, a smile on her face. "George, can I get your help for a minute?"

"What do you need?" George looked comfy on his Adirondack chair, a steamy cup of coffee in hand.

There was a pause, and then Cathy said, "I'd rather not talk about it out here—in the open."

Knox frowned. "Is there something I can do for you?"

Cathy shook her head quickly. "No, thank you. I need George."

With a heavy sigh, George pushed himself off the chair and took his coffee cup in hand. "This could take a while, but I'll be back, Knox. I'm looking forward to more fish talk."

Knox smiled. "I'll be here." He had enjoyed getting to know George under much more relaxed circumstances. The only other time they'd been in each other's company was during his wedding week, when Reina had been a nightmare and everything had been stressful.

It felt different this time, seeing George and Cathy as Merritt's dad and mom. He liked both of them.

Cathy led George into the kitchen, and they disappeared from sight moments after one of them switched off the kitchen lights.

The evening had grown dark, but the firelight illuminated the patio. Knox didn't feel like sitting—he felt like walking and stretching his legs. Ever since last week in the playhouse with Merritt, he'd had this restless feeling he couldn't shake. He hadn't slept well, hadn't been able to concentrate on his work and couldn't sit in one place for long.

With a fleeting glance at the house, wondering where Merritt had taken herself off to this evening, Knox walked across his lawn toward the lake.

His footsteps were heavy on the wooden dock, but not as heavy as his thoughts. Nothing had felt right this week. More than anything, he longed to talk to Merritt and try to convince her to give him a chance, but he wouldn't respect himself if he begged.

Instead, he'd been quiet and sullen. If she wasn't so

close—within reach—maybe he could have pushed his feelings aside easier. Tried to forget about her. But every time he saw her, heard her voice, watched her interact with the girls, it felt like his heart was being torn in two again.

With a sigh, he inspected the boat and then walked to the end of the dock to gaze out at the lake and sky. Millions of stars sparkled overhead, reminding Knox of how vast the universe was and how small he was in comparison. This was his favorite time at the lake, when the day was spent and the night was upon them. It was a time to relax and reflect. But every time he reflected, he just remembered how miserable he felt.

"Knox?"

Merritt's voice came to him from the other end of the dock. He hadn't heard her footsteps across the yard, so when he turned, his heart jumped at the sight of her.

She was silhouetted in the light of the fire. He couldn't see her face, but he had every line memorized. The more he'd come to know her, the more beautiful she had grown in his eyes. She wore a long skirt and a tank top with a cardigan to protect her from the cool night air. Her hair was down around her shoulders, and it blew in the gentle wind off the lake.

Without waiting for him to respond, she walked toward him, her bare feet not making a sound.

"I wasn't sure where you went," she said as she drew closer.

His pulse ticked higher the closer she came. Did she have any idea what she did to him? The longing he felt to draw her close, to pull her into his arms and show her how much he loved her, was so overpowering, he had to put his hands in his pockets to prevent them from reaching for her.

"I'm taking your dad fishing at daybreak." He cleared his throat, forcing his thoughts to return to a safe landing. "I wanted to make sure the boat is ready."

She was finally next to him. He looked out at the lake, focusing on the sound of the water as it lapped against the dock and the call of a distant loon.

"It's so beautiful," she whispered.

He looked down at her as she gazed at the water and wrapped her cardigan tighter around her body.

She slowly lowered herself into a seated position and then reached up and gently took his hand into hers. "Will you sit with me, Knox?"

His heart felt like it would pound out of his chest, but he did as she asked and sat cross-legged, facing her on the end of the dock. She let go of his hand.

They looked at one another for a moment. Though it was dark, he could see her clearly. She studied him for a moment and then said, "I received an email and a phone call this evening."

He didn't know what to say, so he said nothing.

"I was offered a teaching position at both Oakhill Academy and Timber Falls Christian school."

Knox couldn't help but smile. "I knew you would."

"I wasn't so sure." She looked down at her hands and then wrapped her arms around her body. "I have a big decision to make."

"Do you?"

She quickly looked up at him, and he stared at her.

"I thought Oakhill Academy was your dream job," he said. "What kind of decision is there to make?"

Merritt bit her bottom lip for a moment as she seemed to consider what to say. "I spent the majority of my life trying to be the opposite of Reina."

It was the last thing Knox had thought she would say.

"I wanted to live a life independent of her and her choices—but especially of her mistakes." Merritt watched him as she spoke. "I always knew that I was in her shadow, because if Reina was present, all the attention was on her."

Their knees touched as they sat there. Knox wanted to reach out and take her hands, to tell her she didn't need to open up the pain from the past, but he refrained. Both of them needed to heal, and perhaps Merritt had found a way.

"I was an afterthought to most people once they met Reina." Merritt's voice was strong and clear. "I lost many of my friends to her and even a boyfriend or two. But, worse, like I told you before, many of her ex-boyfriends would come to me, and I knew I was second-best in their minds. If they couldn't have Reina, then maybe they could have me and I would get them close to her."

Knox's throat felt tight as he listened to her. "You have never been any of those things in my mind or heart, Merritt."

She nodded. "I believe you now, but my past experiences have told me different. It wasn't until I spoke to my mom earlier tonight that she helped me to see the truth."

Slowly, Knox reached for Merritt's hands. "Remind me to give your mom a big hug."

Merritt smiled, and her dimples shined.

"You could never be my second choice, Merritt." Knox wanted her to understand his heart. "You are my only choice, today and every day for the rest of my life." He knew he was risking everything by telling her how he truly felt. "I love you, with all of my heart and soul, and I will continue loving you until the day I die. I have regretted my relationship with Reina constantly since I realized the mistake I had made— but I don't regret it any longer. If I hadn't met her, I wouldn't have my daughters, and I wouldn't have met you, and that's something I cannot even fathom. You, Blair and Addison mean everything to me."

"And if Brad hadn't broken our engagement and left me at the altar, I would never have come here." She lifted their hands until their palms were facing each other, and she entwined their fingers together. "And that's something I cannot fathom, because I love you, too, Knox. More than I ever thought possible."

Joy filled his heart at her words, and all the awkwardness and uncertainty of the past week melted away. "So, it seems that God created some beauty from the ashes of our pain."

"As only He could." Merritt lowered their hands again. "But it leaves me with a big decision to make. I have two incredible offers on the table."

Knox studied her in the moonlight, his heart pounding hard again, but this time for a whole different reason. "May I present a third offer?"

Merritt nodded.

"Marry me."

She pressed her lips together as tears gathered in her eyes. "You want to marry me?"

He stood and pulled her to her feet, wrapping his arms gently around her. She fit perfectly against him. Warmth filled his chest, and anticipation tightened his muscles. "I don't want to just marry you. I want to spend every day for the rest of my life loving you. I want to raise Addison and Blair and have more babies to fill our home. I want to cheer you on as you teach and celebrate each of your accomplishments. I want to spend our summers doing exactly what we've been doing this summer. I want to sit beside you at church and lie beside you at night. I want to talk with you as we cook supper and fold laundry and make plans." He lowered his forehead to hers. "I want to become one with you, Merritt, in every sense of the word. And I want to choose you over and over and over again for the rest of my life."

She reached up and placed her hand on the back of his neck and drew his lips toward hers.

Her kiss was soft and tender, yet full of a fervency that he felt all the way to his toes.

He deepened the kiss, savoring her passion and love, in awe that she was finally his. It was almost too good to be true. Their kiss lingered. There was nothing to hinder them or hurry them, and Knox enjoyed every moment.

When he finally pulled back, it was only to ask, "What will you choose, Merritt?"

"I'll choose you, Knox." She said it on a breath. "If you'll have me, I'll marry you and stay in Timber Falls to accept the job here."

"If I'll have you?" He laughed, throwing his head back, never knowing as much joy as he did in this moment. He lifted her off her feet and spun her in a circle. "I love you, Merritt."

"I love you, too, Knox."

There was nothing better than hearing her speak those words.

Chapter Sixteen

Merritt sat on the patio the next morning, a coffee cup in hand, as she watched her dad and Knox make their way back to the dock after their fishing excursion. The boat motor was loud as they pulled up to the boat lift and positioned everything to get the boat in place. Knox turned off the motor and then pressed a button to lift the boat out of the water.

Addison and Blair were playing in their sandbox nearby, completely oblivious to the news that Merritt and Knox were about to share with them. They had agreed last night that they wouldn't say anything to her parents until they'd had the opportunity to tell the girls. And since Knox had left before sunrise with her dad to fish, before the girls had woken up, Merritt had been anxious all morning.

If Mom had noticed, she hadn't said anything. She sat on the edge of the sandbox with the girls, helping them build a sandcastle. It was complete with flags they had made from scraps of paper and toothpicks.

Merritt rose from her chair, her pulse pounding, as she met Knox's gaze. His brilliant smile made her knees grow weak, but she did her best to match his smile. All she could think about were his passionate kisses on the dock the night before and the promise of thousands more to come.

Both of the men took a little time gathering their fishing supplies, and they came up to the house with rods and reels, tackle boxes, and a string of fish.

"Look what's for supper!" Dad boasted as he held up the walleye. "Fish fry tonight. I'm cooking."

Mom also rose and wiped the sand off her hands and backside. "Will you need help cleaning them?"

"Yep. I'll gladly take all the help I can get. Knox said I can do it in his garage. He has a sink and counter in there." Dad hardly stopped to address them. Instead, he kept walking toward the garage. "Coming, Cathy?"

"I can help him," Knox said to Merritt's mom.

"Don't worry about it." Mom shrugged. "After thirty years of marriage, he would be helpless without me at his side."

Knox grinned and then turned his full attention on Merritt. "I'm going to go set this stuff in the garage and then I'll be back." He glanced at the girls and then returned his eager gaze to her.

Merritt nodded, feeling more nervous than she needed to be. She knew the girls loved her—and enjoyed her being their aunt—but would they want her to be their stepmother? It hadn't gone well for Mom and Reina. What made Merritt think things would be better for her and the twins? Would history simply repeat itself?

"I want to play in the cottage," Blair said, standing up.

They had started to call the playhouse the cottage.

With Mom's help, they had found a few things in the big house that they had moved to the smaller one yesterday. The girls now had a couple of chairs in the cottage, a small table, a few pictures and even their toddler beds, which they had found in the attic above the garage. They had also moved many of their stuffed animals and dolls, their play kitchen, and their baby doll beds. It was starting to look like a little girls' dream house.

"Okay." Addison also stood and wiped at the sand clinging to her hands and legs. "Then let's take Grandma swimming."

The girls raced away from Merritt. She wanted to call them back but didn't know what excuse she'd give to keep their attention until Knox came back. Instead, she let them run off.

A few minutes later, Knox found Merritt still standing on the patio. She had been wringing her hands as she waited.

"What's wrong?" Knox asked as he came to her and put his arms around her. "You look like you're about to face a firing squad."

Merritt's stomach was turning as she thought about how the girls might react.

"I hope you're not having second thoughts." Knox gently moved a strand of hair off her forehead.

She leaned into him, pressing her cheek against his chest. He was so tall and solid. His presence gave her a boost of courage. "I'm just thinking about how hard it was for my mom to be a stepmother to Reina. The last thing I want is to ruin the relationship I have with the girls."

Knox pulled away, so he could look at Merritt. "First

and foremost, you're family. That will never change. If anything, it'll only strengthen. They've gotten to know you as family. You've never been a threat to them or to their relationship with me. And, most important, they love you dearly. It might not always be easy, but what relationship is? We'll take it a day at a time, together."

"What about when you're gone?"

"Gone? Where am I going?"

"Work trips. It'll just be the girls and me."

He ran his thumb over her cheek, stopping on her dimple. "I've made a pretty important decision myself. I texted my boss from the boat this morning and told him I'm promoting my teammate Caroline. She'll be taking all my trips from now on. I'll be working mostly from here, with a monthly trip to my office in Minneapolis."

"Knox." Merritt couldn't hide the joy from her voice. "Are you sure this is what you want?"

"I've never been more certain of anything."

Knowing that he would be there with her, during the ins and outs of daily life, made her feel a lot more confident in parenting the twins.

"Should we go tell the girls?" Merritt moved away from his embrace and took his hand.

"There's something else," Knox said. "I was out on that boat with your dad for a long time this morning, and, to be honest, I wanted to ask him if we had his blessing."

"You told him?"

"I hope you don't mind."

"Mind?" She shook her head, tears coming to her eyes. "I'm happy you asked him. Unless, of course, he said no."

Knox laughed. "He didn't say no. In fact, he said he couldn't be happier."

"Then let's tell the girls, too."

They walked hand in hand to the cottage, and Knox knocked on their front door.

Blair answered the door with a very grown-up look on her face. "Yes?" she asked. "How may I help you?"

"Could we come in and visit for a while?" Knox asked. "We heard you were new to the neighborhood and wanted to make you feel welcome."

"Daddy," Blair giggled. "It's just me and Addy."

Knox and Merritt laughed as they entered the girls' playhouse. Addy was setting the table for a tea party.

"Would you like to have tea with us?" she asked Knox and Merritt. "We don't have real tea, but we will pretend."

"We'd love to," Merritt said.

She and Knox took seats on the little chairs. Knox's knees came up to his chest, but he didn't seem to mind.

When the girls were ready, they each took a seat across from Merritt and Knox.

"What should we talk about?" Blair asked as she lifted her tea cup, extending her pinkie finger in the air.

"I have something I'd like to talk about," Knox said as he set his teacup down.

"What, Daddy?" Addison asked.

Knox took Merritt's hand in his and looked at his daughters. "How would you like it if Merritt and I got married and she came to live with us forever?"

The girls' eyes opened wide. "Forever?" Blair asked. "To be our mom?"

Merritt watched the girls closely, looking for any signs of anger or resentment.

"Yes," Knox said. "To be your mom and to be my wife."

Without warning, the girls began to cheer, and they jumped up from their chairs to throw themselves at Merritt.

"Yes, yes, yes!" Addy said.

"You're going to stay forever?" Blair asked again.

"Forever, Blair-bear," Merritt said, meaning it with all her heart.

Blair looked up into Merritt's face and smiled. It was slow and tender but also full of incredible joy. "Then I say yes, too."

Knox grinned at Merritt over the tops of his daughters' heads. "That makes three of us."

"Four," Merritt corrected. "That makes four of us."

Merritt had never been so happy or so hopeful in all her life.

It was a beautiful October day. The trees around Tucker Lake had turned red, yellow and orange, reflecting off the smooth surface of the water. It was cool but not unpleasantly so, and for Knox, it felt close to perfection.

He stood near the shoreline, beside the edge of the lake, with Pastor Jacob Dawson, watching as Blair and Addison came down the aisle between all their friends and family who had come to celebrate Knox and Merritt's wedding.

It had been two and a half months since he had proposed and since she had accepted. He would have married her that weekend if she would have said yes, but he knew she deserved the most beautiful wedding he could give her. He had asked if she wanted to wait until the following summer, but she had said a resounding no. Her six-year engagement to Brad had been much too long, and he understood her desire not to wait. Besides, when her parents had left his house after the girls' birthday, she had moved into a short-term rental in Timber Falls, and she had been eager to come back home to the lake. Between getting her kindergarten class ready for her students and starting a new school year, she and Knox had planned their wedding. It was simple yet elegant and reflected both of their personalities.

"Just a couple more minutes," Pastor Jacob said beside Knox. "And then you'll see your bride."

Knox grinned. He couldn't wait.

Several friends from Timber Falls were sitting on the white folding chairs facing the lake. Knox's parents and his sister had come, along with several of his extended family members. Merritt's family and friends had also come from South Carolina.

They were surrounded by everyone who loved them. Exactly as it should be.

A harpist and a violinist played "Canon in D" as Addison and Blair, with Darby on a leash, scattered colorful leaves down the grass path toward Knox. The girls grinned from ear to ear and looked precious in their little autumn-colored gowns with red, orange and yellow rose crowns on their blond hair. When they finally arrived at Knox's side, they each took one of his hands, while Darby was handed off to Grandpa Taylor, and stood there patiently as Merritt's maid of honor, a cousin from South Carolina, walked down the aisle next.

At Knox's side was his brother-in-law, who was

serving as his best man. It was a small wedding party, but they hadn't wanted it to be big. After the ceremony, there would be a light supper and some dancing on the patio. Then, when everyone went home, it would just be Knox and Merritt left for the long weekend. The girls were going to stay at the hotel in town with both sets of grandparents until Monday.

It wouldn't be an extravagant honeymoon, but it was exactly what Merritt and Knox wanted. Just the two of them, alone at the lake, to enjoy the newness of their union. One day soon, they'd go somewhere fun and exotic, but they had all the time in the world.

The door to the kitchen opened, and Merritt and her father appeared. They stepped onto the patio, and all the guests rose to their feet.

Knox's heart pounded hard as he caught his first glimpse of Merritt in her wedding gown. She was stunning. It was the only word Knox could form in his mind to describe his bride. Her brown eyes glowed, and her dimples shined as she walked beside her father down the aisle toward Knox and the girls.

Merritt didn't look right or left as she approached. All she looked at was Knox, Addison and Blair. Her hair was styled in a beautiful updo, with soft tendrils framing her face. She wore a short net veil and an elegant gown. In her hands, she carried a simple rose bouquet that matched the girls' crowns.

When she smiled at Knox, he thought his heart might stop at the pure joy he felt. It didn't seem possible that she could be walking toward him, to marry him and connect her life to his forever.

It didn't seem possible—yet, here she stood.

George gently laid Merritt's hand into Knox's, and then he said, "May God bless and keep both of you."

Merritt kissed her dad's cheek, and then George stepped back to join his wife.

Knox would never remember what Pastor Jacob said that day, but what he would remember was how Merritt looked at him and how much he loved her.

When the vows were spoken and the brief ceremony came to an end, Pastor Jacob said, "I now pronounce you husband and wife. What God has brought together, let no man put asunder." He closed his Bible and said with a grin, "Knox, you may kiss your bride."

With trembling hands, Knox lifted the veil she wore and put his hands on either side of Merritt's face. Then he kissed her soundly, in front of all their witnesses.

Everyone clapped and cheered, and Darby started to bark. When Knox and Merritt finally pulled apart, Knox noticed the girls were clapping the loudest.

"May I present, for the first time," Pastor Jacob said, "Mr. and Mrs. Knox and Merritt Taylor."

There was more clapping, and Merritt smiled up at Knox.

"We did it," she said. "We found our happily-ever-after. Are you still set on giving up on romance for good?"

"Never." He leaned down and kissed his wife again. "The best is yet to come, Mrs. Taylor."

She laughed and took Addy's hand as Blair grabbed hold of Knox's.

"Are we really a family now?" Blair asked him.

"We always were."

"But now we're a forever family, right, Daddy?" she asked.

Knox glanced at Merritt, who nodded. "Forever and ever."

As they walked back down the aisle to start celebrating with their friends and family, Knox couldn't wait to get forever started.

* * * * *

If you liked this story from Gabrielle Meyer,
check out her previous Love Inspired books:

A Mother's Secret
Unexpected Christmas Joy
A Home for Her Baby
Snowed in for Christmas

Available now from Love Inspired!
Find more great reads at www.LoveInspired.com.

Dear Reader,

Summer in Minnesota is my very favorite time of the year. Within a thirty-mile radius of my hometown, we have over three hundred lakes, not to mention countless streams, rivers and ponds—including the Mississippi River, which runs behind my house. Minnesota is known as the Land of Ten Thousand Lakes, but in actuality, we have 11,842. On a given summer day, my children can be in several different bodies of water, playing, floating, splashing and having a wonderful time. I, on the other hand, am usually on the shoreline, keeping an eye on things. I have very much enjoyed writing this story, as well as *Snowed in for Christmas*, set at fictional lakes in my home state. I hope I have been able to capture the beauty and joy of this setting for you to savor, as well.

Blessings,
Gabrielle Meyer

COMING NEXT MONTH FROM
Love Inspired

MISTAKEN FOR HIS AMISH BRIDE
North Country Amish • by Patricia Davids
Traveling to Maine to search for family, Mari Kemp is injured in an accident—and ends up with amnesia. Mistakenly believing she's the fiancée he's been corresponding with, Asher Fisher will do anything to help Mari recover her memories. But can she remember the past in time to see their future?

THE AMISH ANIMAL DOCTOR
by Patrice Lewis
Veterinarian Abigail Mast returns to her Amish community to care for her ailing mother and must pick between her career and the Amish life. Her handsome neighbor Benjamin Troyer isn't making the decision any easier. An impossible choice could lead to her greatest reward...

HER EASTER PRAYER
K-9 Companions • by Lee Tobin McClain
To heal from a past tragedy, Emily Carver and service dog Lady have devoted themselves to teaching children—including handyman Dev McCarthy's troubled son. But Dev's struggles with reading might need their help more. Can they learn to trust each other and write a happy ending to their story?

KEEPING THEM SAFE
Sundown Valley • by Linda Goodnight
Feeling honor bound to help others, rancher Bowie Trudeau is instantly drawn to former best friend Sage Walker—and her young niece and nephew—when she returns thirteen years later. Certain she'll leave again, Bowie's determined to not get attached. But this little family might just show him the true meaning of home...

A FOSTER MOTHER'S PROMISE
Kendrick Creek • by Ruth Logan Herne
Opening her heart and home to children in need is Carly Bradley's goal in life. But when she can't get through to a troubled little girl in her care, she turns to gruff new neighbor Mike Morris. Closed off after a tragic past, Mike might discover happiness next door...

AN ALASKAN SECRET
Home to Hearts Bay • by Heidi McCahan
Wildlife biologist Asher Hale never expected returning home to Hearts Bay, Alaska, would put him face-to-face with his ex Tess Madden—or that she would be his son's second-grade teacher. Their love starts to rekindle, but as buried memories come to light, could their second chance be ruined forever?

LOOK FOR THESE AND OTHER LOVE INSPIRED BOOKS WHEREVER BOOKS ARE SOLD, INCLUDING MOST BOOKSTORES, SUPERMARKETS, DISCOUNT STORES AND DRUGSTORES.

LICNM0222

Get 4 FREE REWARDS!
We'll send you 2 FREE Books plus 2 FREE Mystery Gifts.

FREE Value Over **$20**

Both the **Love Inspired®** and **Love Inspired®** Suspense series feature compelling novels filled with inspirational romance, faith, forgiveness, and hope.

YES! Please send me 2 FREE novels from the Love Inspired or Love Inspired Suspense series and my 2 FREE gifts (gifts are worth about $10 retail). After receiving them, if I don't wish to receive any more books, I can return the shipping statement marked "cancel." If I don't cancel, I will receive 6 brand-new Love Inspired Larger-Print books or Love Inspired Suspense Larger-Print books every month and be billed just $5.99 each in the U.S. or $6.24 each in Canada. That is a savings of at least 17% off the cover price. It's quite a bargain! Shipping and handling is just 50¢ per book in the U.S. and $1.25 per book in Canada.* I understand that accepting the 2 free books and gifts places me under no obligation to buy anything. I can always return a shipment and cancel at any time. The free books and gifts are mine to keep no matter what I decide.

Choose one: ☐ **Love Inspired**
Larger-Print
(122/322 IDN GNWC)

☐ **Love Inspired Suspense**
Larger-Print
(107/307 IDN GNWN)

Name (please print)

Address   Apt. #

City   State/Province   Zip/Postal Code

Email: Please check this box ☐ if you would like to receive newsletters and promotional emails from Harlequin Enterprises ULC and its affiliates. You can unsubscribe anytime.

Mail to the **Harlequin Reader Service:**
IN U.S.A.: P.O. Box 1341, Buffalo, NY 14240-8531
IN CANADA: P.O. Box 603, Fort Erie, Ontario L2A 5X3

Want to try 2 free books from another series! Call 1-800-873-8635 or visit www.ReaderService.com.

*Terms and prices subject to change without notice. Prices do not include sales taxes, which will be charged (if applicable) based on your state or country of residence. Canadian residents will be charged applicable taxes. Offer not valid in Quebec. This offer is limited to one order per household. Books received may not be as shown. Not valid for current subscribers to the Love Inspired or Love Inspired Suspense series. All orders subject to approval. Credit or debit balances in a customer's account(s) may be offset by any other outstanding balance owed by or to the customer. Please allow 4 to 6 weeks for delivery. Offer available while quantities last.

Your Privacy—Your information is being collected by Harlequin Enterprises ULC, operating as Harlequin Reader Service. For a complete summary of the information we collect, how we use this information and to whom it is disclosed, please visit our privacy notice located at corporate.harlequin.com/privacy-notice. From time to time we may also exchange your personal information with reputable third parties. If you wish to opt out of this sharing of your personal information, please visit readerservice.com/consumerschoice or call 1-800-873-8635. **Notice to California Residents**—Under California law, you have specific rights to control and access your data. For more information on these rights and how to exercise them, visit corporate.harlequin.com/california-privacy.

LIRLIS22

She leaned back, watching him.

Curiosity about this man who could make the best of
a difficult childhood—and who actually owned a garlic
press—flashed through her, warm and intense. She didn't
want to be nosy, shouldn't be. His childhood wasn't her
business, and she ought to be polite and drop the subject.

But this man and his son tugged at her. The more she
learned about them, the more she felt for them. And maybe
part of it was to do with Landon, with his being the same age
her son would have been, but that wasn't all of it. They were
a fascinating pair. They'd come through some challenges,
Dev with his childhood and both of them with a divorce,
and yet they were still positive. She really wanted to know
how, what their secret was. "Did you grow up in the Denver
area or all over?"

"Denver and the farm country around it." He slid the
bread into the oven. "How about you?"

"Just a few towns over on the other side of the mountain." Indeed, she'd spent most of her life, including her married life, in this part of the state.

He didn't volunteer any more information about himself and Landon, so she didn't press. Instead, she leaned down and showed Landon Lady's favorite spot to be scratched, right behind the ears. Now that they weren't working anymore, he was talkative and happy, asking her a million questions about the dog.

It was hard to leave the kitchen, cozy and warm, infused with the fragrances of garlic and tomato and bread. Her quiet home and the can of soup she'd likely heat up for dinner both seemed lonely after being here. But she had her own life and couldn't mooch off theirs. "I'd better let you men get on with your dinner," she said and started gathering up her books.

"You want to stay?" Dev asked.

The question, hanging in the air, ignited danger flares in her mind.

The answer was obvious: yes, she did want to stay. But an Unwise! Unwise! warning message seemed to flash in her head.

Spending even more time with Dev and Landon was no way to keep the distance she knew she had to keep. As appealing as this pair was, she couldn't risk getting closer. Her heart might not survive the wrenching away that would have to happen, sooner rather than later.

Don't miss
Her Easter Prayer *by Lee Tobin McClain,*
available April 2022 wherever
Love Inspired books and ebooks are sold.

LoveInspired.com